NANCY WARREN

CROCHET AND CAULDRONS

VAMPIRE KNITTING CLUB
BOOK THREE

Cover Design by Lou Harper of Cover Affair

ISBN: ebook 978-1-928145-52-3

ISBN: print 978-1-928145-51-6

Ambleside Publishing

INTRODUCTION

Every family has annoying relatives; mine just happen to be undead.

My Grandmother, Agnes Bartlett, used to own Cardinal Woolsey's knitting shop in Oxford then died and left her shop to me, without informing me that she wasn't actually dead. She's a vampire and part of the world's strangest craft circle – the Vampire Knitting Club.

As you might imagine, this means she's free to interfere in how I run the business that used to be hers. She's trying to teach me to knit and it's not going well. She's also trying to teach me how to be a witch, since it turns out I'm from a long line of witches. Another tiny detail about my family that no one ever told me, along with the long-lost witch cousins I recently discovered.

But I'm learning. I've got my family spell book, my black cat familiar, some powers that sometimes scare me, and an interesting new group of friends.

My archaeologist parents are coming to visit and bringing me a gift I could do without.

So, to recap, I run a knitting shop and I can't knit. I'm a beginning witch who can't always control her cat, never mind her magic, and my love life is as tangled as the last sock I tried to knit. Oh, and for some reason, I keep getting involved in murder investigations. Good thing I have my vampire knitters to help sniff out clues.

Get the origin story of Rafe, the gorgeous, sexy vampire in *The Vampire Knitting Club* series, for free when you join Nancy's no-spam newsletter at NancyWarrenAuthor.com.

Come join Nancy in her private Facebook group where we talk about books, knitting, pets and life.
www.facebook.com/groups/NancyWarrenKnitwits

CROCHET AND CAULDRONS

CHAPTER 1

"Good afternoon, Mrs. Winters," I said, walking into the corner grocer at the top of Harrington Street, in Oxford. It was convenient, only up the block from where Cardinal Woolsey's Knitting Shop was located.

Our little corner of Oxford was my favorite part of that ancient city. There was one college on the street, but it wasn't famous. There were no world-class restaurants or fancy hotels. No celebrity had been born or died here. It wasn't even in the oldest part of the city. What Harrington Street had, was rows of tiny shops and houses that had stood there for about two hundred and fifty years. And one of them was mine.

I'd only been running Cardinal Woolsey's for a few months and I was still discovering new quirks and oddities in the neighborhood—and that was just the people! Of course, since I was both young and American, I often had to explain how I came to own a quaint, old knitting shop. The easiest explanation, and the truth, was that I'd inherited the shop when my beloved grandmother died.

The slightly more complicated explanation, also true, was that before she was all- the-way-dead, one of Gran's vampire friends turned her. So, I ran the shop with a great deal of interference from a group of bored know-it-all vampires who were crazy good knitters.

"How's business, Lucy?" asked Mrs. Winters. She was inclined to be nosy.

"Fine. I'm thinking of branching into selling designer knitted garments, possibly on the Internet." The vampire knitting club turned out the most incredible work at warp speed and I hoped that if I could keep them busy enough, they might have less time and energy to interfere in my life. It was a faint hope, but I was clinging to it.

"That's a lovely sweater you're wearing," she said, peering at me closer. "Did you knit it yourself?"

I swallowed the urge to snort. My attempts to knit were about as good as my track record at keeping an assistant. Pitiful. The sweater I wore was gorgeous. A deep purple background with an indescribable, but beautiful, geometric pattern of diamonds and squares in complimentary shades, it had been made by Doctor Christopher Weaver, a local GP and vampire. The vampires took turns knitting me sweaters, shawls, and dresses to wear in the store. Every day I turned up in something amazing, which I usually only wore once, as there was always another new creation waiting for me to slip into. That's why I was thinking of branching out into ready-made items.

"I need a new assistant, though," I said, holding up the advertisement I'd made. "Do you mind if I pin the job posting on your community board?"

I'd also put the ad online and I'd posted a help wanted

sign in my front window, but everybody in the neighborhood checked the community board at Full Stop, the grocer's. It was the best place to find a violin teacher, a roommate, or a job.

However, pinning a notice up always had a price. Especially as I kept putting up the same one: "Shop Assistant wanted at Cardinal Woolsey's Knitting Shop. Must be an experienced knitter with retail experience." I went through assistants the way an allergy sufferer with a bad cold went through tissues.

I waited. Sure enough, she raised her brows in fake shock. "Good heavens. Another assistant?" She leaned across the counter, past the display of lottery tickets and a plastic basket of mini packs of Chocolate Buttons and Jelly Babies, all ready for Halloween. But her voice was so piercing I'm sure they could hear her at the top of the Radcliffe Camera. "It's very important to keep consistency. Rapid staff turnover isn't good for your business's reputation." She smiled at me in a very patronizing way. "I'm sure you don't mind me giving you a hint, my dear. Only, I've been in business a great deal longer than you have."

I could have told her that my first assistant had been a psychopath, my second assistant had freaked out after seeing my supposedly dead grandmother wandering around the shop, and my third had gone back to Australia to be with her boyfriend, the murderer, but I held my tongue and tried to look grateful for the unwanted advice.

Then, as though belatedly remembering how I had come to lose my third assistant, she said, "Of course, it's all been so dreadful with that fuss at the tea shop."

It takes a very special person to call two murders a fuss.

I smiled sweetly. "Can I put up my notice?" It was a Sunday afternoon and I was spending my only day of the week off doing catching-up chores, like vacuuming, and advertising for a new assistant.

"Yes, of course, dear. And I'll keep my eye out, too, for the right person. What sort of employee do you have in mind?"

I knew exactly the sort of person I wanted. I could picture her in my mind. "I'm looking for a middle-aged woman, perhaps someone whose children have grown and is looking for part-time work. She has to be an excellent knitter, of course, have some experience in sales, and if she's got teaching experience that would be even better. She must be available to work Saturdays." I pictured a plump woman who wore cardigans that she'd knitted herself.

She'd be motherly, the kind of person who could dispense life advice as easily as she could turn a sleeve or knit a picture of Santa and the reindeer into a child's red sweater. *Jumper*, I corrected myself mentally.

I felt certain she was out there, my fantasy knitting shop assistant. Until she showed up, I was making do on my own with sporadic assistance from some of the vampire ladies who had never been known locally when they were alive. Naturally, my grandmother was desperate to be involved, but I only let her help with the stock-taking and tidying up once the store was closed and I'd pulled the blinds.

Having tacked up my notice and purchased fresh bread and milk for me, and half a dozen cans of tuna for Nyx, my black cat familiar, who is very particular about her diet, I walked the short distance back to my shop, my reusable cloth shopping bag swinging from my hand. Now that my chores were done, I was looking forward to an afternoon studying magic spells, with the help of my family grimoire. My witch cousin and great aunt kept encouraging me to join their coven, but I was hesitant to do so, with so few witchy skills to offer.

The truth was, I seemed to get thrown into things I wasn't very good at. For instance, I owned a knitting shop, and I couldn't knit. I'd tried and tried. Gran said I didn't focus properly, but I found it very difficult to keep my attention on a couple of metal sticks and constantly looping wool around them while keeping count. I couldn't figure out how anyone kept their focus. My creations, whether attempts at scarves, socks, or sweaters, all ended up looking like variations of the sea urchin or hedgehog family. Sometimes I thought I should invent a line of knitted hedgehogs. I could really go to town.

Gran said I came from a long line of illustrious witches. I didn't know what my descendants might say of me, in the future, but I didn't think they'd use the word illustrious. My potions didn't turn out, I'd forget my spells halfway through, and I tended to blow things up. Not on purpose.

The only reason I half believed I was a witch was that my cat was clearly a very powerful familiar. I called her Nyx, after the goddess of night and daughter of chaos, and she was well named. She was the smartest cat I'd ever known, and when she was around things happened. I didn't think she'd stay with me if she didn't believe I had potential, though sometimes she looked at me sideways out of her green eyes and I could tell she was having second thoughts. If I ever stopped feeding her the best tuna Full Stop grocers had to offer, and tried to put cat food in her dish, I thought she might take off for greener pastures.

However, I did have dreams that turned out to be significant, though not always at the time, and when my emotions were engaged I made things happen that were mysterious even to me. Not much to hang my pointy witch hat on, but it was all I had.

How could I possibly turn up to the local witches coven and present myself as one of them? They'd sweep me out with their magic broomsticks. And who could blame them? But it was lonely being the only witch I knew, apart from my cousin and great aunt. So, I was determined to practice until I got my skills to a level where I felt the other witches might accept me. It was a bit like practicing baseball all summer in the hopes of making a team when school started. Of course, that hadn't worked out for me. After a summer of practicing, I couldn't ever seem to connect the baseball bat with the ball, and my pitching was worse.

I was so busy having glum thoughts about my future as a witch, that I failed to notice two people standing in front of Cardinal Woolsey's. It was a man and a woman, middle-aged and looking as though they had been standing there for a while. The first thought that went through my mind was how tedious it would be to get rid of them. If I explained that I was the owner, and that we were closed, they'd have some sob story about how they desperately needed wool today because... They'd expect me to open up for them. It's amazing how people had taken the phrase 'the customer is always right' to mean the retail world should revolve around their desires.

I was contemplating simply walking on past, as though my destination were elsewhere, when I realized these two were very familiar. As soon as I drew close enough to be certain, I dropped my bag onto the sidewalk and ran forward with my arms wide open. "Mom, Dad, I can't believe you're here."

Jack Swift and Susan Bartlett-Swift were rock stars in their field, which happened to be ancient Egyptian and Sudanese archaeology. Being a husband and wife team added glamor to their work as professors. Outside of that, no one had ever heard of them. They'd spent as much of their lives in the Middle East as they had in the States, which is why I ended up spending so much time in Oxford with my grand-mother, when I was growing up.

"You're both so tanned, you look as though you've been on a Caribbean cruise," I teased.

Dad said, "We hit a sandstorm coming through Giza. Oh, but it's good to see you, Lucy." He enveloped me in a hug. Then I turned from him and hugged Mom, who wore a coat that looked like a giant sleeping bag. It was late October and chilly, but to a woman used to the heat of the desert, it would be freezing here.

I found my keys and opened the door into the shop, which seemed easier than walking them around to the proper entrance to the flat, which was around the back and down a lane. I realized, then, that Mom hadn't been here since her mother, my grandma, had passed away. This was going to cause complications. Because, of course, her mother wasn't actually dead, she was more in the undead category. I wasn't certain it was a good idea for my parents to discover that Gran was a vampire. And yet, she wandered around whenever the shop was closed, and, sometimes, disconcert-ingly, when it was open. I wasn't sure I'd be able to stop her from showing herself to her daughter and son-in-law. But I'd cross that rainbow bridge when I came to it.

Mom and Dad travelled light, with a wheeled bag and a backpack each. I carried Mom's bag for her and led the way upstairs to the flat, where I now lived. I turned on lamps to chase away the darkness of the afternoon. Then, I took Mom's puffy winter coat and Dad's ancient wool bomber jacket and hung them in the closet.

"But, what are you doing here? And why didn't you tell me you were coming?" I looked from one to the other. "Was it political unrest?" That was usually the only thing that catapulted them out of a dig once they were, well, dug in.

Mom classed political unrest with the weather and inadequate funding as irritations that prevented her doing her job properly. My parents were single-minded in their fascination with digging up history. They knew much more about the goings-on in the ancient world than about the modern one.

But Dad looked at Mom, who shook her head. She looked sort of confused. Had she been drinking on the plane? Mom rarely drank so I wondered if a couple of cocktails at thirty thousand feet had sent her loopy. Something had.

"I wanted to see you, Lucy." She put a hand to her brown hair, liberally streaked with gray, which had grown past her shoulders since I'd last seen her. "And I need a haircut."

Mom was not a woman who left her job and went to another country to get her hair cut. Apart from looking buzzed, Mom seemed in great shape. She wore her usual uniform of oversized cotton shirt with chinos and desert boots. Since she refused to wear trifocals, she was wearing her medium distance glasses and had both her reading glasses and her long distance glasses tucked into the pocket of her shirt. She never wore makeup and her only jewelry was a plain, gold wedding band.

My Dad wore pretty much the same uniform, only his shirt was a faded blue denim. He'd given in to trifocals and his new glasses were pretty trendy since I'd helped him pick them out. I'd inherited my blond, curly hair from him, though his was more silver than gold. Years in the desert had given him a rugged, windswept complexion. He looked like an older Indiana Jones.

They were brilliant archaeologists, and hopelessly impractical about everyday things. I adored them both. "You should have told me you were coming!"

"Mom wanted to surprise you." Also, odd behavior. Mom hated surprises.

"Well, I'm surprised all right. I'm so happy to see you." Then, I laughed. "I don't know what we're doing standing here in the living room. Sit." I offered them tea. My mother laughed softly. "You're becoming as English as your grandmother. Don't you have any coffee?"

"Of course, I do." I went into the kitchen and got busy preparing coffee. Mom followed me in. I said, "This must be so hard for you. It's the first time you've been back since Gran died."

"Harder for you, I think. I'm so sorry you got the shock of arriving here and finding out she was gone. It must've been awful."

Oh, she had no idea. Not only had I found my supposedly dead grandmother wandering around, but, with the help of the vampire knitting club, I'd had to solve her murder. Naturally, Mom knew nothing about that. "I got through it."

She didn't waste any time getting to the Mom question I was already dreading. "I understood you staying at the beginning, honey, but why are you still here? You're twenty-seven years old. What are you doing running a knitting shop?"

I'd sort of fallen into this new life, partly because Gran had left the shop and the flat upstairs to me, but mostly because I'd grown to like it so much. As crazy as it sounded, I looked forward to the biweekly meetings of the vampire knitting club. They were a strange bunch from very different eras, but they were my friends. I enjoyed running a shop more than I'd imagined, and, if I ever learned to knit, I'd be really good at it.

"You'd be surprised, Mom. Knitting and crochet aren't just for little old ladies, anymore. I get students in here, young men and women, there's even a club that meets in pubs to knit. They're called the Oxford Drunken Knitwits." So there.

"Are you making any close friends?"

Okay, so most of my friends were celebrating birthdays in the hundreds, but I'd stopped thinking of them that way. "I'm busy with the shop, but I'm getting out. I'm thinking of taking a class on how to run a small business, and as soon as I get time, I'm going back to yoga classes. You know what Oxford's like. There are lectures, concerts, theater, book launches, and pub quizzes on all the time, here."

I put three mugs of coffee on a tray along with a plate of homemade gingersnaps. Gran knew they were my favorites and she made them for me regularly. When Mom saw them, she put a hand to her heart. "Mum used to make those for us. You found her recipe. I never knew she'd written it down."

I smiled and fervently hoped Mom didn't ask me for the heirloom recipe as I hadn't got a clue how to make them.

When we were settled, Mom and Dad side by side on the chintz sofa and me on one of the overstuffed chairs, she went back to her previous one-sided conversation. "Are you sure you aren't lonely?"

"Never. Besides, I have a roommate." Then I raised my voice. "Nyx?" I called out. Normally, the cat hung out with me whether I was home or in the shop. It was strange she wasn't here now, getting to know Mom and Dad. Especially as she'd be a good distraction from the third degree I was getting.

Mom and dad looked at each other. Dad said, "Who's Nyx?"

"My cat. I don't know where she is. She usually loves meeting new people."

"That's so nice," Dad said. "You always wanted a cat or a dog growing up. We couldn't have pets because we were away so much."

I hunted around and found Nyx, upstairs, sitting by the window in my bedroom. I normally left the window open for her, but, because it had been cold earlier, I'd shut it.

"Come and meet my parents." I picked her up and carried her back down and into the living room, where my parents were drinking coffee, both looking jetlagged. I felt Nyx stiffen in my arms and pull back. I nudged her towards my dad and he held out a hand and stroked her on the head.

"Nyx? Glad to see you haven't forgotten your classic mythology."

My mom was more of a cat person and she leaned over and stretched out a hand saying, "Oh, what a sweet kitten." I leaned forward so Nyx could jump onto her lap. There was nothing my cat loved more than to be fussed over. However, Nyx suddenly had some kind of a fit. She hissed and twisted in my arms, her tiny, but sharp, claws fully extended and leapt onto the carpet, scratching me as she went. Then she ran at full speed back upstairs.

My mother looked surprised and a little hurt. "She's not very friendly, is she?"

I was staring after the cat, puzzled. "I don't know what's going on with her, today. Maybe she needs to go out." I excused myself and went back up to the bedroom.

Nyx glared at me through narrowed green eyes, before turning her head and pointedly staring at the window, waiting for me to open it. My arms were smarting where she'd scratched me. She was always so gentle. "What's up with you?"

She gave an annoyed meow. I had known her long enough that I could interpret the many moods of her meow. This one was angry. She wasn't the only one. I opened the window. "I hope you'll have better manners when you return." As soon as I had the window open, she shot out so fast I was afraid she'd tumble down to the ground. However, with an agility that always amazed me, she jumped to the branch of the old cherry tree and made her way rapidly down to the small back garden.

When she was safely on the ground, she turned and looked up at me. And my beloved cat and familiar narrowed her eyes and hissed at me.

CHAPTER 2

I rubbed my sore arm, still feeling puzzled by her odd behavior, and went back to my folks. My dad had his head tipped back on the sofa, asleep. Mom seemed wide-awake though, and she still seemed kind of buzzed.

She smiled at me. "I'm so glad to see you. We've missed you, honey." She glanced around. "You haven't changed much in the apartment, have you? I'm glad in a way. That means you're not committed to staying."

I probably would have modernized the place a bit, but I didn't want to hurt Gran's feelings. Besides, I was too busy. I really didn't want to talk about my future plans half-an-hour after my parents arrived, so I settled on, "I've missed you, too." Especially now that Gran was gone. Sometimes, I wanted an older woman I could talk to, someone I could trust. Not that Gran was gone, exactly, but the longer she was a vampire, the more I noticed her losing touch with the little concerns of daily life that are part of being human.

Mom glanced at Dad in a secretive manner. He had his mouth open and was making tiny little gasping sounds in his sleep. She lowered her voice. "Let's go up to your room, honey. I have something for you."

She looked both mysterious and excited, and I happily followed her up the stairs to my room. I loved presents. She shut the door, then listened, to make sure Dad was still asleep, before giving a little nod.

She came over and sat beside me on the bed, opened her handbag and then withdrew her cosmetics bag and unzipped that. Finally, she took out an object in a well-worn leather pouch and passed it to me. "The minute I touched this, I knew I had to bring it to you."

It was such an odd choice of words, that I glanced at her. She had a glow of excitement about her and her eyes were fixed on the bag, waiting for me to open it. So, I did. I slipped my hand into the bag and withdrew something that looked like a hand mirror. On closer inspection, I realized it was a hand mirror, but a very, very old one.

It was beautiful. The mirror, itself, was round, about four inches in diameter, and made of a metal that had dulled with time. I guessed it was bronze. However, it was the handle that drew my attention. It was gold and featured the stylized head of a woman. Her face was painted, and reminded me of the bust of Nefertiti, with large dark eyes, made of obsidian, that seemed to be looking right at me.

The mirror looked like something you'd see in museum, very much like something my mother and father might have discovered in a dig. There was even some hieroglyphic writing inscribed into the handle.

"Mom, it's beautiful. Is it a replica of something that you found?" I'd often seen copies of famous artifacts in museum gift shops around the world. Sometimes Mom or Dad would point out the ones that had been copied from objects they had personally found. I always thought they were torn between pride at having their work so honored, and horror that something so valuable and unique could ever be mass-produced. However, some of the copies were very good. This one certainly was. The bronzed mirror part was a little clouded. It was such a perfect re-creation that it must've been very expensive.

Mom sighed and reached out with her index finger. "Look at the exquisite detailing on the hair. This is really a most extraordinary piece."

I was starting to get a very peculiar feeling. Mom wasn't acting like herself and, now I looked closer, I saw that her pupils were dilated, like she was high on something. "Did Dad help you pick this out?"

She shook her head. "No, dear. And let's keep this our little secret, shall we?"

My mom and dad did not keep secrets from each other, especially not about anything related to the ancient world. My unease increased. "Mom, this isn't an actual historical artifact, is it?"

My mom laughed, then. A delighted trill that sounded nothing like her. "I found it, and, you know what they say, 'finders keepers.'"

When archaeologists were paid by universities, museums, and government funding bodies to discover ancient treasures, the finders keepers rule did not apply.

Was she playing some kind of trick on me? I looked at her, but she was transfixed by that mirror. Mom did not joke about the sanctity of the artifacts they discovered and she was a strong and insistent voice in the attempt to save vulnerable ruins from pirates and marauders. She and my dad had worked hard to stop looting and destruction in war-torn areas. She would never take something from a dig. Never.

She reached over for my hand where it was still clutching the mirror. "It was strange, but the moment I unearthed this mirror, I knew I had to bring it to you. I haven't let it out of my sight since then and now it's safely in your hands, I can finally breathe a sigh of relief."

I was glad someone was breathing sighs of relief, because my anxiety was rising. "Where, exactly, did you find it?" I asked, trying to keep my voice casual.

"We're working in the valley of the kings. This was in the burial chamber of one of the minor wives of Senakhtenre Ahmose. You'll remember, he was Pharaoh of Egypt in the seventeenth dynasty, mid sixteenth century, BCE to us, of course." Mom and Dad always used the more scholarly, BCE — Before Common Era— instead of BC, though they meant the same thing.

I did the math in my head, as I always had to do when Mom or Dad threw out historical dates. If my quick calculation was correct, this wife had been buried around thirty-five hundred years ago.

"There was the usual bric-a-brac in the burial chamber: alabaster urns holding the internal organs of the dead queen, ivory combs, jewelry, and tools for the next life. But this mirror, this mirror was something special and because you're so special I brought it for you as a present."

I was stunned. There's no other word for it. First, my mom, the famous archaeologist, did not term precious relics found in a tomb as 'bric-a-brac' and second, she would never, in a million years—or thirty-five hundred years—pilfer from a dig.

I didn't want to accuse my mother of stealing and I didn't want anyone else to find out and accuse her, either. All I could think was that she was suffering some kind of memory lapse or perhaps heatstroke. Or could she have picked up an exotic virus that was making her act crazy? I wanted to discuss her condition with my father. And then, maybe get her to a doctor for a check-up.

Taking a treasure from an ancient burial site was not only a crime but it would get Mom fired from the job she loved. Possibly my father, too, because he'd been an unwitting accomplice..

My mother, oblivious to my thoughts, was still studying the mirror. "Just look at the exquisite hieroglyphics. Do you remember how to read them?"

This was beyond bizarre. Now I was getting a pop quiz on hieroglyphics? Of course, I knew how to read them. When you spent weeks and weeks in an archaeological dig, there wasn't a lot else to do. As I looked at the beautifully carved shapes I obediently tried to make sense of them. I studied the tiny figures, the birds and mythical animals. "It looks like a protection spell."

"Very good. Let's hear you read it aloud."

My ancient Egyptian was pretty rusty, plus there wasn't really a standard pronunciation, but I did my best. Reading the words aloud took me back to times I'd spent in the desert as a teenager, when I'd longed for the Internet, friends, sometimes even electricity.

Archaeology is very exciting when you're an archaeologist, but to me, as a teenager, it was about the most boring occupation there was. I'd never been allowed to help with anything important. The grad students got to do the fun stuff, if you could call using tiny brushes to shift sand and debris off of ancient chunks of stone, fun. Mostly, all I'd done was run errands. One year, I was given high school credit for a history course, so Mom had made me study hieroglyphics. That had been cool once I got into it. The tiny drawings and stick figures began to take on meaning and drew me into the ancient world in a way Mom's and Dad's lectures never did.

I never slept well when I was on those digs. Not only because the accommodation was pretty basic, but because my dreams would get worse. I'd always been plagued by nightmares, but I'd ended up dreaming that I was one of the people we were currently digging up, which was rather disconcerting. What sixteen-year-old wants to go to sleep hoping her boobs will grow bigger and wake up in the middle of the night experiencing the world through the eyes of a two-thousand-year-old mummy?

I got to the end of the incantation, with Mom making me re-pronounce a couple of the words I got wrong. The minute the final word left my mouth, I knew something bad had happened.

How could I have been so stupid? I was a witch. I knew the power of spells. This mirror was so old that I'd assumed any magic it once held, or any spell it might have carried, would be as mummified as the woman who'd owned it.

I was wrong.

The mirror grew warm in my hand, so I felt like I was holding hands with another living human.

My mother's eyes rolled back in her head and she fell backwards on the bed. I'd have gone to her, but I couldn't look away from the surface of the mirror. It was emanating a strange blue light that shimmered.

As I stared, the wavering opaque surface became clearer and clearer. It was like my scrying mirror, except that when the surface stilled, I was looking at the image of a very young and very beautiful woman. And she was staring back at me.

Her eyes were dark brown and rimmed with kohl. Her eyebrows were thick and painted black in the fashion of Egyptian women of three thousand years ago. She had full, sensual lips, a long, elegant neck, and delicate bone structure. She wore her long black hair in complicated braids that wrapped around her head. If she'd stepped out of that mirror and I lent her something to wear, we could have gone clubbing.

I was so freaked out, I tried to drop the mirror to the ground, where hopefully it would break, but I couldn't let go. The mirror's handle was clinging to me, and the more I tried to loosen my grip, the tighter it held on.

The young Egyptian woman was looking right at me, as though she were real. Even though I was freaked out, I said, aloud, "You are so beautiful." She was, too.

"You are beautiful, also," she said, politely. I really did try and drop the mirror then. I even shook it, the way you'd shake off a dog biting your ankle.

"Please," she said, and she sounded as freaked out as I was. "Who are you? What is this place?"

I stopped shaking the mirror and looked at her once more. I had some rudimentary knowledge of ancient Egyptian, but she wasn't speaking her native language. She spoke mine. The words were said in English, but with a slight, exotic accent.

What do you say when an apparition in an ancient mirror asks your name? I gave it. "My name is Lucy Swift. Who are you?"

"I am Meritamun. Daughter of Amenemhat, High Priest of Amun. And you are in grave danger."

Not me. It was my mom, currently passed out on my bed, who had filched a priceless antiquity that had magic powers. I'd heard of cursed, Egyptian tombs, who hadn't? "You've been separated from your gravesite. I'm very sorry about that, and I'm going to get you back where you belong." So please don't send disease and pestilence to my family.

She shook her head, looking impatient. "It is too late. Having me in your hand has put you in great danger."

"What about the person who actually found you? Are they in danger, too?"

Amazingly, she shook her head. "Only the person who has conjured me. He will use my power to destroy you. That which was meant to protect, now kills. I wish it could be different. You must prepare yourself."

And then the picture went fuzzy, as though we were communicating online and the connection were getting lost. She began to fade away. "Wait!" I cried. "Who is out to destroy me and how do I stop them?"

But with a final look of sadness she disappeared, and the mirror was once more only a mirror.

CHAPTER 3

"Mom? Mom! Are you all right?" I sat on the bed and chafed my mother's hands. She was breathing regularly and seemed to be sleeping naturally. After a minute or so, her eyes fluttered open and she looked at me, puzzled. "Lucy? What are you doing here? I thought you were in Oxford?"

Oh, I was seriously going to get her to a doctor. "I am in Oxford. So are you. You and Dad came to visit me, remember?"

She sat up and rubbed her temples. "No. I don't remember. I feel so strange."

And she had the behavior to back it up. "What's the last thing you do remember?"

She squinted, as though she were being interrogated, but that was her expression whenever she was thinking deeply. "It was such an exciting day. We found the tomb of one of the minor queens. I was deep inside the tomb. I remember something catching the light and glittering. Of course, nothing ever does glitter when it's been underground for that long,

21

not even pure gold. I bent down." She shook her head. "That's the last thing I remember."

The spell on that mirror had led her straight to me, and the woman in the mirror, whoever she was, seemed to think that spell could destroy me. But why? And why had my mother felt compelled to hand-deliver death to her own daughter?

"And then you suddenly decided to visit me? In the middle of this exciting find?"

She put her hand to her head once more. "I wonder if I've got a touch of fever. It's all a blur. Perhaps that's why your father insisted we come. Because I was ill."

"Let's ask him."

I put the mirror on the bedside table and my mother didn't even glance at it as we both left the room.

Dad had napped through the entire incident, but when Mom called his name, he jerked awake. "Excellent idea. I'll call the college right away." Then he blinked fully awake and yawned. "I think I dropped off."

"Dad? Why did you and Mom suddenly decide to visit me?"

He looked at my mom and back at me. "We've been planning to come since your grandmother passed away, but we were going to wait a few weeks until we'd catalogued this new find. However, your mother suddenly decided she had to see you immediately. It was strange, because we were in the middle of something rather exciting, but your mother is a woman of strong determination.

"I agreed to come along, as there are some colleagues here in Oxford I'd very much like to see. Besides, we've been worried about you. We wanted to make sure that you're living the life you've chosen rather than one your grandmother may have chosen for you."

That all sounded perfectly reasonable, except for the part where they had run out in the middle of a dig, and my mother had brought some kind of death-cursed mirror with her.

I asked, "Were you two together, your last day on the dig?"

"No," he said. "I was preparing a revised budget, asking for further funds since we'd discovered another tomb that we didn't know was there. Looking for funding is one of the things I hope to do here in Oxford. I also hope to find some promising graduate students who might like to spend a term out there with us. Anyway, your mother came running in, her eyes all bright and her cheeks flushed, to say we must come home immediately to see you, Lucy."

My mother had been listening to this. Now, she nodded, as though a tricky question had been answered. "I must have had a touch of fever. I don't remember any of that, or the journey here. If I had flushed cheeks and bright eyes, I'm sure fever was the reason."

He looked concerned. "You have been behaving strangely. Let's get you to a doctor while you're here."

"Yes," she said. "It's probably time I had a check-up. In fact, we should both have one."

I wondered whether I should tell them about that mirror. Dad clearly didn't know anything about it and I had a feeling that Mom didn't remember. But, if I told them about the mirror, then I'd have to tell them about the magic spell that surrounded it. The thing was, they didn't know I was a witch. And they didn't know Gran was a vampire or that we hosted knitting circles for the undead several times a week. In the delicate state my mother seemed to be in, I didn't think revealing all that shocking, new information was a very good idea. If she'd fainted from the power of that mirror's spell, finding out her daughter was a witch and her mother a vampire might be the end of her.

However, a woman in an ancient mirror had warned me I was in terrible danger. I needed help, probably of the supernatural kind, and fast. I also needed all the information about that dig site, and the tomb, that they could give me. "Who was in the tomb, exactly?"

My dad leaned forward and placed his hands palm to palm, a sure sign that he was about to launch into lecture mode. "Well, that's a very astute question, Lucy. What's exciting about this find is that there are a number of skeletons in the tomb, and they all appear to have died at the same time."

I swallowed. "You mean there was some kind of epidemic that killed a bunch of people at once?" Please, let it be that.

Dad shook his head. "This was a lesser wife's tomb, but obviously she was a favorite of the pharaoh, based on the elaborate burial. We believe there were a number of retainer sacrifices. These would be people the young queen believed she'd need to serve her in the afterlife. Her servants. They may have volunteered to be sacrificed in order to continue to serve her in eternity, or they may not have been given the choice. It's very difficult to say."

I had to sit down. "How, um, were they killed?"

"There was no trauma to the head or bodies that we've been able to find. We suspect they were poisoned, though they could also have been strangled. We hope to do extensive testing to find out." He winked at me. "But my money's on poison."

I felt suddenly hot and claustrophobic. I was remembering my nightmares, back when I'd visited them on site. So, it seemed, did Dad. "Are you okay, honey? You've gone pale. You used to look like that in Egypt after you had a nightmare. Gosh, you used to have some powerful nightmares when you came to the dig site. Remember?"

I was not likely to forget. Even now I recalled the feelings of terror that had me sitting up in bed and yelling.

"She was always a sensitive child," Mom added. "Knowing she was surrounded by ancient graves, gave her ideas."

In my dreams, I'd seen the sarcophagi, the burial chambers, but from the inside. Thinking of the girl in the mirror, I had to ask, "Were there any young women sacrificed with the queen?"

"Definitely. The average age of the skeletons is twenty years old and there are more females than males in this particular tomb."

Twenty years old was about the age of the girl in the mirror. I shuddered. "Are there any curses associated with this particular queen? And her burial?"

Dad and Mom exchanged a glance, then Dad said, "There are always curses. Things like, 'If anyone disturbs this tomb, they will die a violent death,' that kind of thing. But I don't remember anything out of the ordinary. Do you, honey?"

Mom did the face-scrunching, deep thinking again. "This young queen was particularly superstitious. She kept her own priestess nearby, a young girl who could interpret her dreams and was said to be able to foretell the future."

"What was her name?" I tried to be cool, but my voice came out wobbly.

Dad shook his head at me. "Lucy, honey, there must be twenty mummies in there. I can't remember all their names. We've barely started cataloguing the find."

"Meritamun," Mom said. "She was the Daughter of Amenemhat, the High Priest of Amun. It would have been a great honor for her to join the royal household. No doubt the high priest gave her some tips on interpreting dreams and giving the kind of vague prophecies that today's fortune tellers still rely on." She mimed holding a crystal ball and put on a deep voice. "You will meet a tall, handsome stranger. You will go on a journey." She laughed and shook her head. "People were as gullible then as they are now."

Gran had said that Mom had magic in her and refused to face it. I remembered her saying that it made my mother vulnerable to dark forces who might use her latent powers against her. Had that happened in Egypt?

Something had, and the upshot seemed to be that I was now in possession of a cursed mirror. The Meritamun that I'd met wasn't predicting I'd meet a tall, handsome stranger, or that I'd go on a journey. I could have coped with either of those prophesies, no problem. Unfortunately, she predicted great danger. And, gullible or not, I believed her.

MY PARENTS WERE tired and jetlagged, so we decided to go to the local pub for Sunday roast. It would be a late lunch and early dinner. I could probably have scratched together a simple supper, but I didn't want them bumping into Gran.

Until I'd warned my undead grandmother that her non-believing daughter was in the house, I needed to physically keep them apart.

I sent Rafe a text, letting him know they were with me and asking him to keep Gran out of sight. I was certain that one day, Mom would find out that her mom was a vampire, but she was too fragile right now. Having been bewitched and used as a human mule to transport a cursed mirror, I didn't think Mom was ready for more shocks.

The Bishop's Mitre was at the top of Harrington Street, across from the grocer, and served proper British pub food. Steak and kidney pie, fish and chips, macaroni and cheese, sausages and mash, and a few dishes for the vegetarians. They also did a roast Sunday lunch, one of my favorite British traditions. On Sundays the pub offered roast beef and York-shire pudding, with roast potatoes and veg, or roast pork, or chicken. There was a nut roast for the vegetarians.

My folks bundled up again in their warm coats. I was worried about being too warm in my thick sweater, so swapped it for a gorgeous red shawl, hand-knit by a former policeman, now vampire, named Theodore. I wore it with my best jeans and a simple white shirt.

The pub was busy with family lunch parties, and groups of friends. I'd lived in the neighborhood long enough, now, that I recognized a few people. There was Bessie Yang, a yoga teacher, and her friend, Dr. Amanda Silvester. I made sure to say hello, and introduce my parents, thinking Mom might be more receptive to seeing a doctor she'd met socially.

We settled in a quiet booth and my dad went up to the bar to deliver our orders. Red wine for me, white for Mom, and a British beer for him.

Over lunch, we caught up. They asked me for my news from home, by which they meant Boston, and I did the same. Since our circles weren't that similar,, we had different gossip to share, though it was all second hand, as none of us had been back home for months.

"Any news of Todd?" Mom asked at last. Todd had been my boyfriend for two years, and I think my parents had assumed, rather than hoped, that I'd marry him. But Todd had turned out to be cheating on me with a woman he worked with. I'd walked in on them, in one of those clichés of modern relationships that you think will never happen to you, until it does. My best friend, Jennifer, and I had rechristened him The Toad after that.

"Jennifer said the woman he was cheating on me with, dumped him. He sent me a couple of emails, but I deleted them."

My dad said, heartily, "Better to have loved and lost, and all that."

"Todd was looking for an old hoodie he couldn't find." I'd have liked to think he'd wanted me back, just so I could kick him to the curb. Yep, I'd spent two years of my life, that I was never getting back, with a man like that.

"Plenty of fish in the sea," my dad said, moving on to the next platitude on his list.

"Really, Jack," Mom said. "You have no idea what it's like for these young people today. It's all 'swipe left, swipe right.' How do they ever find love?"

"Come to Egypt," was Dad's next bright idea. "There's barely ever working Internet, and more young men than you can shake a stick at."

"The only problem is, they're all archaeologists." I was

teasing, but not really. I loved my parents, but I couldn't live that life.

After dinner, we'd all succumbed to dessert. Sticky toffee pudding for me, bread and butter pudding for my mom, and my dad, no sweet tooth, ordered cheese and biscuits and another beer.

We were home by seven and caught up on the news on TV. By nine they were both yawning.

Since I'd arrived in Oxford, I'd been sleeping in the guest room, where I'd always slept when I visited Gran. Even though her room was larger, I hadn't moved in there. It seemed wrong when she was still around, not that she used the room. Gran lived in a gorgeous subterranean warren with a nest of local vampires. However, since it was located right underneath Cardinal Woolsey's, I saw her frequently. I'd been happy to stay in my old room, and so I prepared Gran's room for Mom and Dad.

I wasn't certain if Mom would be able to sleep in her own recently-deceased mother's room, but she said it would comfort her. So, I put fresh sheets on the bed and found some clean towels and wished them a good night. It wasn't long before all sounds of activity ceased. I waited half an hour and then eased open the door and peeked in. They were both sound asleep.

I went back into my own bedroom and, unfortunately, the mirror was still sitting on the bedside table, exactly where I'd put it. I hadn't experienced some sort of temporary insanity.

I didn't want to pick it up with my bare hands, not after the way it had gripped me before, and refused to let go. I slipped on a pair of gloves before replacing the mirror into the leather pouch Mom had transported it in, and then into one of Gran's cloth knitting bags. Then I texted Rafe that I urgently needed to see him.

Rafe Crosyer was a well-respected expert in antiquarian books. He was a fellow of Cardinal College and a consultant to libraries and book collectors all over the world. He was also a vampire.

I didn't want him coming upstairs and I didn't want all the other vampires to know what had happened, so I asked him to meet me downstairs in the shop. He arrived minutes after I texted him. How he travelled so fast, when his home was several miles away, was a mystery I preferred not to probe. I let him in and took him straight into the back room where we held the knitting circle. I switched on the light and we settled into two of the chairs, facing each other.

As always, when I was around Rafe, I felt hot and cold at the same time. He was quite swoon-worthy to look at, like one of those dark, dangerous heroes the Brontë sisters wrote about. Heathcliff could have been modeled on him. In fact, perhaps he was.

Vampires don't blink as often as the rest of us, so it was slightly unnerving the intent way he stared at me. It made me fidget and wish I'd done a better job of combing my hair, or making sure my clothes were neat and that I'd bothered to freshen my makeup.

He, on the other hand, always looked perfect. His black wool trousers seemed perfectly creased, as though he'd never sat down in them, his sweaters, of the finest cashmere, never seemed to pill like everybody else's did and his black hair was always well groomed. His gray-blue eyes studied me. "Something's happened to upset you."

The understatement of the year.

"Like I said in my text, my parents arrived, today."

He nodded. "And you're afraid that Agnes will show herself."

Right now, that was the least of my problems, although it was a concern. "Mom is still grieving her loss; I don't think it would be good for either of them to see each other, not quite yet."

"I agree with you. Agnes is still transitioning, and it's hard for her with so many loved ones around. I wish we could convince her to move away for a while, but she's not ready."

We'd had this conversation before. I wanted to do the right thing for Gran, but the truth was, I still needed her. Before she was turned into a vampire, she'd been a witch and she was the person I most relied on to teach me witching skills. She was also always handy with good advice on running the knitting shop. "I'm not ready, either."

"I know. Shall I see if I can find an excuse to send her away, just for a few days? Until your parents are gone?"

"Do you think she'll go?"

He considered the question. We both knew my grandmother was as stubborn dead as she had been alive. Maybe more so. "I'll get Sylvia to explain to her why a trip would be best, and then I think she'll go. You can add your encouragement at the knitting club meeting tomorrow night." Sylvia was Gran's best friend, and the person who'd turned her into a vampire. That made her Gran's maker, I think is the term. It meant they were strongly bonded and Gran pretty much did whatever Sylvia told her to do.

I liked Sylvia. She was a glamorous, silver-haired former film and stage star, but her diva qualities hadn't died with her. She could be bossy, unreasonable, and vain. Since she had no reflection, I was pretty sure she used Gran as her personal makeup artist.

And thinking of mirrors... "That's not all that's bothering me." I picked up the bag and, using my still-gloved hand, pulled out the mirror and showed it to Rafe. "Do you have any idea what this is?"

He was accustomed to handling rare books with linen gloves, so he didn't seem particularly surprised to find me doing something similar. He pulled a pair of cloth gloves out of his pocket and put them on. He reached out his hands. "May I?"

I didn't imagine a death curse could do much damage to someone who was already dead, so I let him take the mirror from me. Naturally, Rafe understood hieroglyphics and, much more fluently than I had done, he read the protection spell aloud.

I flinched when his deep voice had recited the last of the protection spell. I could feel the chair back pressing against my spine and my heart began to pound.

But nothing happened. No blue light, no three-thousand-year-old woman warning of evil and destruction on its way. It seemed that special treatment had been just for me.

CHAPTER 4

"What can you tell me about it?" I asked him, as he sat, studying the mirror.

He answered my question with a question of his own. "Where did you get this?"

I huffed in irritation. "I asked you first."

He shook his head at my childishness, as he often did, but he also answered my question. "It's Egyptian, obviously, I'm guessing between 1400 and 1700 BCE. It's gold and obsidian. The surface of the mirror looks like bronze. Someone high-born or royal used it and they were someone very special, as it's been inscribed with a protection spell." He glanced at me. "Your parents would be the ones to tell you all about this. They're the experts."

I told him the whole story, then, relieved to be able to share the freakish experience. I started with the moment my mother arrived, looking as though she'd been drinking, through me saying the spell out loud, exactly as he had, while holding the mirror, and everything that happened to me after

I did. He made me repeat the entire story a second time. "And this woman spoke to you. In your own language."

"Yes. I felt like Luke Skywalker when Princess Leia pops out of that robot and asks for his help."

Rafe stared at me blankly. Honestly, he could tell in an instant that an artifact was three thousand years old and Egyptian, but recent cultural events escaped him. I shook my head. "Star Wars."

"Popular culture bores me," he said.

One day, I was determined to show him what he was missing. But not today. "Why would me reciting a protection incantation cause this woman to tell me I'm in terrible danger? Isn't the whole point of a protection spell to save you from danger?"

"I admit that has me in a puzzle, too."

"And why me? This thing has been buried in sand, presumably for a very long time, why would my mother come across it and suddenly feel compelled to bring it to me?"

"Another excellent question." He looked at the mirror again. "She said it caught her eye as it was so shiny."

"That's right."

"I wonder if she didn't actually dig it up, but it was placed there for her to find."

"You just found a way to make this worse. You're saying she might have been deliberately targeted?"

"I'm only speculating. I have no idea."

I asked him the one that was really bothering me. "Do you think I'm in danger?"

His dark, calm eyes looked directly into mine. "I think you'd be very foolish not to take the warning seriously."

So not what I was hoping he'd say.

"As I said, your parents are the experts in that area. Can't you show it to them?"

How was I going to show it to them, without causing a whole lot of problems? If Mom even remembered she'd brought the mirror with her, which I doubted, my dad would freak out. If Mom didn't remember, then they were both going to wonder how I had come into possession of such a rare thing. When I explained it to him, Rafe shook his head. "I don't know. I'll do some research and see what I can find out."

"Great. And you'll get Sylvia to take Gran away for a few days?"

"Yes. At least I can take that worry off your shoulders." He looked at me as though he'd like to take more of them.

In the end, I snapped a picture of the mirror with my phone and decided to show it to my dad in the morning and see what he had to say.

The next morning my parents woke up rested and full of plans. My dad was heading out to a meeting of Egyptologists at his old college while my mom went to hers to see about recruiting some grad students.

Fortunately, Mom left first, and, when I had my dad to myself, I asked, "Can you tell very much about an artifact from a picture?"

"I can do a better job with the actual, physical object, but you can tell quite a bit from a good photograph. Why do you ask?"

I told him that a friend had inherited this mirror and didn't know what to do with it. And then I showed him the picture on my phone.

My dad studied the picture carefully and kept increasing

the size of the photograph and looking at small details of the mirror. He was a very careful researcher. Finally, he looked up. "Where did your friend get this?"

Provenance is a big deal when you deal in antiquities. Rafe and I had already made up a story that seemed plausible. "My friend's great-great-grandfather bought it in Cairo in the late 1800s. It's been in her family ever since."

He shook his head, looking annoyed. "So many treasures were pillaged in that time. It's shameful. Well, you can tell your friend that, assuming this is genuine, it's an extremely well-preserved lady's mirror from the Middle Kingdom. I'd say this mirror is from around 1500 BCE."

"Wow. Thanks."

He sat back. "If this is genuine, it should really be in a museum. If your friend wants to donate the mirror, I could arrange it, and a plaque, acknowledging the gift, would be displayed alongside the artifact."

"Thanks, Dad. I'll tell her."

Then he rushed off to his meeting and I sat wondering whether Rafe could be right. Had the mirror been deliberately dropped at my mother's feet and somehow been enchanted so that she brought it to me? The idea was preposterous but so was the situation.

I had half an hour until I had to go down and open the shop and so, probably foolishly, I shut myself in the bedroom and retrieved the mirror. It was like a sore tooth I couldn't leave alone, but kept poking at with my tongue. I read out the incantation once again. I reasoned that I'd already been threatened with death, how much more could be done to me?

I'd hoped that nothing would happen, like when Rafe had read out the spell. I wasn't so lucky. As before, after I read out the incantation, the mirror began to glow blue and the same young woman appeared on the wavy surface of the mirror. She seemed surprised to see me. "You are still living. I am so glad."

Well, that would be two of us. "You have to tell me who sent you. And why am I in danger?"

She looked so sad. She said, "I was once like you. A good witch, with the power to help, but I was tricked by an evil one, and trapped here. Now, he uses my power to find others like me. I am helpless to stop him."

"But, can't you refuse?"

"I have tried. It is impossible. My only hope is escape or death. It is what I dream of, what I have dreamed of for centuries now. While I have watched strong and wonderful witches be destroyed, all over the world."

"And how would you escape?" I side-stepped the death wish, hoping she was being dramatic.

She smiled again, sadly. "You would have to break the spell. But no one has been able to break it in more than three millennia."

And I'd been a witch for about two months. I didn't like the odds. Still, I didn't like to see one of my witch sisters stuck inside a mirror, forced to destroy her own kind, either. "I want to help you," I said. "Tell me everything you can. Who were you in life?"

She looked down and then back up at me. Her large, dark eyes were solemn and I felt rather than saw the echo of fear in them. "My queen was the youngest of the pharaoh's wives and the prettiest. She was a great favorite, but she was also ambitious and determined to be his number one wife."

I thought the real number one wife might have had something to say about that.

"The other wives did not like or trust her. And we, her servants, had to be careful. Spies were everywhere in our household. I was her priestess and personal advisor. Naturally, I urged caution in her dealings with the pharaoh and, especially, his other wives and their households. But, she was very ambitious and very determined. She believed she could have anything she wanted as soon as she bore her husband a son." She sighed. "I was to ensure she bore a son, by using my powers."

That had to be a precarious position to be in. "Did she know you were a witch?"

She smiled. "We did not use that term, then, but yes, she knew."

"And did she have a son?"

"Oh, yes. But after that she became obsessed with taking what she considered her rightful place beside her husband."

"What happened?"

She shook her head. "I could see darkness ahead and I tried to warn her, but she did not want to listen. She went to another priest. A man who promised her everything. But he had his price."

I had a bad feeling I already knew where this was going. "And that was?"

"His price for helping her, was me."

Yep, pretty much what I'd guessed.

"Why? Why would he want you?"

"Because I have a special gift. I'm more sensitive than most to being able to feel my sisters. Other women with gifts. Sometimes I connect with men, but usually it is women. His power comes from darkness and evil. But he takes shapes that are pleasing or seem innocent. He wants to destroy all of us. He uses me to lead him to his next prey."

"How did he capture you?"

"He tricked my poor queen. She believed she would get everything she wanted, but she was too eager, and paid no attention to those who perceived her danger. She was poisoned, along with most of her servants. I was put under a spell and cursed to live in this mirror, seeing the faces of others who will die, because of me."

"But, it wasn't your fault."

"And yet, I am the means of killing my own kind. You have so far escaped destruction, but you must be ever vigilant."

I promised I would try, and then she faded away, but not before I'd seen a tear slip down her cheek.

I MADE certain the mirror was well-hidden before I went down to open the shop that Monday morning, I was surprised to find a man standing outside, already waiting. It was still five minutes before opening time, but he looked so sorry for himself that I invited him in. He looked to be in his mid-sixties, with a round face and sorrowful eyes. He wore a yellow cardigan—not hand-knitted, but from some-place like Marks & Spencer's. Underneath the sweater I glimpsed a white dress shirt and a striped tie. He had on navy blue trousers and brown loafers that looked recently polished. He carried a leather attaché case. I suspected he was on his way to work and had popped in to buy his wife, perhaps, the wool she'd run out of as she was knitting a sweater.

I smiled at him. "Good morning. Can I help you?"

"Yes," he said. "I've come about the job."

"What job?" Was there some appointment I'd made and forgotten? Some work I was having done around the flat or shop? I tried to think of anything I'd had upcoming, but I came up blank.

To my surprise, he pointed to the notice hanging in my window.

"Oh, you mean the job here, at the shop, to be my assistant?"

He nodded. He did not look thrilled at the possibility of working as my assistant. He was far from the picture I'd had in my head of my ideal candidate, but I knew how well some of the men who came into the shop, including the male vampires, could knit. If he fit my criteria he might be perfect.

"I brought you my CV," he said, unzipping the attaché case and handing me a two-page resume. I glanced at it and saw that he'd been a career accountant. There was nothing on the two pages about retail sales, knitting, or any kind of crafts. I glanced up. "Do you knit?"

"No," he said. And then he sneezed. He pulled a handkerchief from his pocket and, even as I was saying 'bless you,' he was already sneezing again, explosively.

"Do you have any retail sales experience?" I asked.

He shook his head. His eyes had begun to water and they were becoming red around the rims.

"Are you all right?"

"I'm allergic to wool." He blew his nose. "Also cats."

I didn't quite know what to say. I glanced around at the

baskets of wool, the balls and skeins in shelves lining the walls. "You'll find a lot of wool in a knitting shop."

He nodded, looking grimly satisfied. "That's what I told my wife. She said, 'I don't care, I've got to get you out from under my feet. You apply for every job there is, and don't come back until you've got one.'" He sneezed again "I just retired, you see, and she's not used to having me underfoot. She says I need to get a job."

"But not here," I said, trying not to laugh as he sneezed again. "You'd be miserable."

He nodded. "Thank you for understanding." At least I thought that was what he said; he was so stuffed up by this time he sounded as though he had no nasal passages at all and his voice was reduced to a croak. "But you'll remember my name, Ned Cruickshank, in case she comes to check?"

That poor man. What he needed wasn't a job, but marriage counseling. "Of course, Mr. Cruickshank. I hope you find what you're looking for."

He nodded, sneezed again, and scuttled out.

I watched him leave, hoping he'd feel better soon. Out on the sidewalk I heard him blowing his nose with gusto. At least his severe allergic reaction had told me that Nyx was hiding around here, somewhere.

"Nyx?" I called. Even though the shop was quite small, there were any number of places a small, wily cat could hide. I found her under the cash desk. I coaxed her out, and, after playing with her by trailing a piece of wool over her until she pounced, over and over again, we managed to restore our relationship. Though it cost me a ball of wool, since she'd pretty much shredded it to pieces playing cat and mouse.

Once she'd relented towards me, she curled up in her

favorite spot—a shallow pottery bowl of assorted wools in the front window. People often stopped to take her photograph as they passed the window. She was so darn cute. I wondered how many Facebook posts and Instagram updates featured my adorable cat. I'd made sure to surround her with brochures that featured my shop address, figuring I'd use her for free advertising.

Once she'd rolled around until she was comfy, I said, "That mirror freaked you out, didn't it? It's freaking me out, too."

I would need to consult my family grimoire and see if there was some kind of spell that could release the girl in the mirror. I'd slept poorly as I kept seeing her face. She'd looked so sad. I imagined being trapped for millennia and forced to do evil and decided it must have been hell.

Still, I was only a baby witch, I should probably work on protecting myself before trying to save another witch from some very powerful evil. Even as I tried to convince myself I was only going to save myself, I knew I'd at least attempt to rescue that poor girl.

I was still preparing the shop for the day, and hadn't yet had a single customer, when a young guy walked in. He glanced around the shelves, looking slightly confused, as though he'd intended to walk into a mountaineering or outdoor store and accidentally stumbled into a quaint knitting shop.

He was tall and rugged, with sun-streaked shaggy blond hair, and reddish stubble covering his cheeks and chin. His warm hazel eyes twinkled and the skin around them was prematurely wrinkled, presumably from staring into the sun. He was wearing faded jeans and a cream denim shirt open to reveal a muscular chest. He was young, gorgeous, and did not look as though he had any business in my shop. Once more, I said, "Can I help you?"

"Too right, I've come about the job," he said in a strong Australian accent.

Was Mrs. Winters playing some kind of trick on me? I couldn't imagine who else would keep sending these entirely improbable candidates my way. Still, there were strict laws about discrimination in hiring practices that meant I couldn't turn this serious hottie away simply because he didn't look like my idea of a knitting shop assistant. Besides, the idea of spending a few minutes with him wasn't entirely unpalatable. I said, "Do you knit?"

When he grinned, his teeth were big and white. If he took a bite of something he'd mean it. "I can knit up an open wound, a good skill to have in the desert."

"Yes," I agreed. "But not the most important quality when working in a knitting shop."

He looked at me as though I was the crazy one. Then, he glanced around and seemed to appreciate that he actually was inside a knitting shop. "Have we got our wires crossed?"

"I think that's the least of what's been crossed."

He scratched his head and pulled out his phone. "I'm sure this is the right address. To apply for going on the dig? In Egypt?"

The penny dropped. *My parents!* "Could I see that?"

"Sure." He handed me his phone and, sure enough, there was a notice on one of the university Internet forums describing the dig and asking interested graduate students to come to this address. I explained that it was my parents he wanted, not me, and that he should come back after five

43

when my shop was closed and my parents would likely be here to interview him. I suggested that if he knew anyone else who was thinking about applying, they should also come after five o'clock.

"No worries," he said. "It's a nice shop, though. If I were the knitting sort—" Then he glanced around again at the walls crammed with colored wools, the knitting patterns and magazines, the wall of notions and shook his head. "Naah. Could never stand to be cooped up. It's the open air for me." With a cheerful wave, he opened the door to leave. Then, he stood back and held it open for an older woman who was just entering.

"I'll be with you in just a moment," I said, rapidly texting both my mom and my dad that they needed to specify in their advertisement that anyone wishing to join the dig should come by after five o'clock tonight and please to make sure they were here to interview the perspective archaeology students themselves.

While I was doing this, the woman was walking around, looking at my various wares. It was nice to see someone in my knitting shop this morning who actually looked as though they could knit. She was probably in her mid-to-late-sixties, with gray hair that was turning to white. It curled softly around her face. She wore a pink cardigan that was clearly hand-knit, featuring a complicated pattern of flowers around the border. With that she wore a mauve woolen skirt, what looked like support hose, and black, orthopedic shoes. She carried a capacious handbag and, when she paused to look at my shelves, she rested her hands atop her belly.

"Can I help you?"

"I'm very much hoping I can help you," she said, with a

sweet smile. "I saw your advertisement for an assistant and I'm here to apply for the job."

"Really?" I must've sounded as delighted as I felt. It was so nice to find someone applying for the job who looked, in fact, exactly like the assistant I'd pictured in my mind.

"You haven't filled the position?"

I didn't want to appear too anxious, so I said, "I've had a couple of applicants already this morning, but I haven't made any decisions yet. I have to ask you the most important question, though. Do you knit?"

She chuckled at that. "My dear, I've been knitting for fifty years. I've knit sweaters for myself, my mother and father, and my brothers, and then later baby clothes and blankets and layettes of all sorts. I also crochet, do needlepoint, and cross stitch, weave on my own loom, and I can card, dye, and spin my own yarn."

I, who owned Cardinal Woolsey's, could barely tell a knit from a purl. "Well, that's certainly impressive. Did you knit the sweater you have on?"

She glanced down, as though uncertain what she was wearing. "Oh yes. I designed it, too."

Inside my head, a tiny me was fist bumping and yelling, *Yes!* "Do you have any retail experience?"

"I ran my own knitting and crafts store in Cornwall. I did that for about twenty years, but I got tired of running the business. I moved here when my third grandchild was born. I wanted to be close to my daughter and her family. But, now, the youngest has started school and, frankly, I'm a little bored. When I saw your ad, I was quite pleased, because this is exactly the kind of thing I like to do."

She was so perfect my feet wanted to tap. I had to hold

them still. "I don't suppose you've ever taught knitting classes, have you?"

"Oh yes. I taught through my own shop and then I taught young girls through an after school program. I still hear from some of them, little dears."

My only fear was that the money would be too little for her and I said as much, telling her the salary I could pay her in an apologetic tone. But, to my surprise, she said that would be fine. "I've plenty of money from my late husband's life insurance. Rest his soul. I need to fill my time more than I need the money."

I felt churlish even asking for references, but given Mrs. Winters' opinion that I hired poorly, I decided to ask for them, assuring Mrs. Percival—Eileen—that it was purely routine.

She opened her bag. "I understand perfectly, my dear. Here's a CV and on the bottom are the names of two people who would be happy to vouch for me. You have a beautiful shop here, and I think we could be very happy working together."

So did I. I took her resume and, with a 'thank you very much for stopping by' said I would let her know the next day.

After she left, and I didn't think she could see me through the window anymore, I picked Nyx up and said, "We did it! We found the perfect person!" And then I proceeded to dance the cat around the room until we were both a little dizzy.

CHAPTER 5

When the vampire knitting club met that night, we didn't hold it in my shop, as usual, since my parents were upstairs. We moved it to the underground apartment complex that housed Gran and many of the local vamps. Some, like Rafe, had their own homes, in his case an ancient manor house, but they congregated here, under my shop. This was their clubhouse.

It was comfortable in the deep, plush chairs and couches, but it wasn't the same, somehow, as being upstairs in the shop. Possibly because of the location change, there was a smaller group than usual. Gran was there, with her best friend and maker, Sylvia. Rafe was there, with Alfred, and Christopher Weaver. Silence Buggins, looking like she'd stepped out of a Victorian novel, sat primly, her corset holding her stiffly upright. Clara, a lovely older woman who didn't say much was present, but her friend Mabel was visiting friends in Scotland. Hester, the eternal, moody teenager was present, yawning in the corner. Theodore, the former police officer, had gone to Budapest. He'd gone into

47

business tracking down lost treasures and seemed to be enjoying the challenge.

Gran couldn't settle. She kept changing her seat, complaining the light wasn't right. She couldn't seem to concentrate on her knitting. I glanced at Sylvia to see if she knew what was wrong and she motioned me to follow her. We went under a Gothic stone archway into a hallway that led, I assumed, to bedrooms. I'd never been all the way down these hallways.

She pushed her sweep of silver hair behind her ears, where I noticed she was wearing a stunning pair of art deco diamond earrings. Sylvia was the most glamorous vampire I'd ever met. Tonight she wore a midnight-blue silk pant suit.

"Your grandmother's very upset. She wants to see her daughter, but Rafe's forbidden it."

"I should think so," I whispered back. I was shocked. Even I knew that, now Gran was a vampire, she couldn't show herself to anyone. I only knew about her, because I'd stumbled on the information. She was still part of my life, and I was grateful every day to have her, but Mom wasn't like me. She was a scientist, a woman who believed only in the rational, the provable. If she saw Gran, she'd freak out. And not in a good way.

I'd been worried sick that Mom or Dad would accidentally bump into Gran, who had a bad habit of sleepwalking. I lived in constant fear that she'd show up in the shop in the middle of the day, this woman who was dead. "We have to get her to leave town," I said. "Rafe said you'd talk to her."

Sylvia nodded. "I've already tried, but she says you need her."

I bit my lip. I did need Gran. But not now, when my

parents were around. The stress of trying to keep them apart would be too much. "If I can convince her I don't need her, will she go?"

"I think so, but her feelings will be hurt."

I thought for a minute and then snapped my fingers. "I've got it. What we need to do is franchise."

Sylvia raised her penciled brows. "Franchise?"

"Not for real, obviously, but what if there was another knitting shop somewhere that was for sale? Or even an empty store that could one day be a yarn store. You and Gran could go and check it out. Maybe there's another city that has a lot of vampires who like to knit? We could find a sympathetic human and open a second knitting shop. Run a sister vampire knitting club."

She touched her throat, where a matching art deco necklace glittered. "Do you know, Lucy, that's not a bad idea."

I put up my hand, traffic cop style. "Wait, wait. I'm not suggesting we actually do it, but if Gran thought we were going to, she'd feel important. Like she was helping me."

Sylvia smiled her movie star smile. "That's a very good idea."

"Good. We just need a location. Somewhere where Gran will be happily occupied for a couple of weeks."

She tapped her fingernails against her collarbone. "Dublin, perhaps. I've got lots of friends there, and I've been meaning to visit. I can keep your grandmother occupied, and I'm sure we can find a suitable shop for your expansion plans." She tilted her head. "Or some small town in Connecticut, perhaps, or Vermont. Or Massachusetts. You'd like that. A second shop in the United States."

"But I'm not opening a second shop. This is only a ruse, to get Gran out of the way for a couple of weeks."

"Of course."

When we told Gran about our idea, she brightened up. I could tell she was still sorry not to be able to see her daughter, but she was excited at the idea of traveling to an interesting place and researching a second shop location. "What an adventure it will be." Her white hair was coiled neatly in a bun at the back of her head, and she patted it now as though afraid she might have mislaid it. "I often used to think of expanding, of course. But I was too old. But you're so young, Lucy, so full of energy and possibilities. You could do anything. You could have a chain of shops all over the world. Money's no problem, of course. All the vampires who've been around for a few centuries are extremely rich. You'd have venture capital coming out your ears."

I didn't want venture capital, or anything else, coming out my ears, but I was happy to see Gran looking so much more cheerful.

Sylvia said, "We'll start in Dublin. That way, we can take the Bentley." She turned to me. "Your grandmother's very partial to the Bentley."

"I'm happy to go to America, too, Sylvia. I haven't been there in years."

"We'll start in Dublin, then fly to New York. I'll bet you've never flown first class, Agnes. You'll enjoy that."

By the end of the meeting, I was saying goodbye to Gran. They were going to leave that night. I was sad to see her go. I'd become accustomed to her being close to me, ready to give advice, but I knew this was the right thing for all of us. I hugged her goodbye.

Gran held me close and whispered, "Find a way to tell Susan how much I loved her, and how proud of her I am."

"You left her a letter, remember?"

She brightened up at that. "Oh, I did. That was clever of me."

Then, I narrowed my eyes at her. And, for the first time, realized I'd been duped. "Gran! You wrote those letters to me and Mom after you were turned, didn't you?"

She shrugged. "I'd always meant to, but one never realizes one's time will be up so soon. Anyway, I was given an opportunity to tidy up my affairs. Not everyone is so lucky."

"Mom was so happy when she got your letter. It meant a lot to her."

She sighed, looking sad. "But, she's not like you. She's not open. So, I must leave and make sure she doesn't see me." She hugged me once more. "Take good care of her for me."

It was such an odd thing to say. But I agreed I'd do my best.

Sylvia came to say goodbye and handed me a silver-wrapped package.

"What's this?" It wasn't my birthday or a gift-giving occasion that I knew of.

She smiled. "Just a little something for you to wear. Save it for something special. A date with a special man, perhaps."

The way things were going, the next ice age would set in before whatever was in the box saw any action, but I thanked her anyway.

Rafe walked me back upstairs, as he usually did when I'd been visiting my vampire friends. He said, "That was a good thing you did, giving Agnes a compelling reason to leave. She knew she had to go, but she was having trouble. Now, she's got something to look forward to."

"Good." We reached the wooden stairs that led up to the back room of my shop. "Rafe, they won't actually buy a shop, will they?"

He shook his head. "Where your grandmother and Sylvia are concerned, I wouldn't care to hazard a guess."

It seemed I no sooner got rid of one problem than another popped up. My life was becoming like a game of Whack-a-Mole.

When I got back upstairs to my flat, I opened the silver-wrapped gift and drew out the most exquisite knitted top. It was made out of sapphire-blue silk thread, with long, bell sleeves, and a vee neck that showed just a hint of cleavage. There was something else in the package. A small, jewelry box. When I eased open the lid, I saw a silver chain with a star-shaped diamond hanging from it. I thought, at first, that it was a crystal, but when I looked closer I was certain it was a real diamond. And no doubt the chain was platinum, or white gold. Tucked in the tissue, so I'd nearly missed it, was a note. It said, "Dear Lucy, I never had a daughter. If I did, I'd have wanted her to be like you. Wear this, for me."

"And that makes it impossible for me to return it to her," I said to Nyx, who regarded me from the windowsill.

Which was quite a good thing as I really wanted to keep it.

My new assistant, Eileen Percival, started Wednesday. Her references had been superb and I was really looking forward to having her help me. She arrived five minutes early for work, in a purple and pink cardigan. I had no idea what stitches she might have used, but they were clearly complicated. If she were only undead, she'd be a great addition to my vampire knitting club.

She wore a purple tweed skirt, support hose and the same, sensible, black shoes. She had very fine skin and it looked to me like she was wearing face powder and a rather pretty pink lipstick. Looking at her made me want to buy wool and knitting needles, and I couldn't even knit. I was very excited about my new hire.

After she'd put her purse on the shelf I indicated behind the cash desk, she rested her hands on top of her belly and looked at me, expectantly. I said, "I thought for today you might want to become familiar with our inventory, look through the patterns we have and I can show you how the cash register works."

"That would be fine," she said.

She checked each basket methodically and asked intelligent questions, some of which I could actually answer. Then, I showed her how to use the cash register, which took no time at all as she'd used something similar in her own shop.

I felt that I had to explain how I came to be running a knitting shop, when I obviously couldn't knit, so I told her about my grandmother and how she'd left me the shop and flat when she passed away. Eileen listened while tidying up the shelves. When I'd finished, she said, "But how is it your grandmother never taught you to knit?"

"She tried, but I have no aptitude."

She turned her head and gave me a droll look. "I don't want to argue with my employer, not on my first day, but that's nonsense, dear. Every girl can learn how to knit. I'd be happy to teach you."

Her words might be a bit sexist, but if she could teach me, I could forgive a little knitting-shop sexism. She glanced around. "Since the shop is currently empty, why don't we begin now? Then you can decide if you want me to teach classes for you."

"Sold," I said. I went to one of the knitting magazines I'd flipped through in a bored moment and showed her a sweater I loved. It looked simple enough, being all one color and without any fancy stitches. "What about this?"

She came over and looked over my shoulder. When she grew closer I noted that she smelled of lavender and old-fashioned roses. "No. That's too complicated for a beginner. We'll start very simply and you can progress to knitting jumpers when you've learned the basics."

I was disappointed, but tried not to let it show. "Fine."

"We'll begin without a pattern. Get yourself some needles and I'll find the wool."

I picked out a medium sized pair of needles and she fetched a ball of bright red wool. When she saw my needles she shook her head. "Bigger, much bigger. We want to start with nice, fat needles so you can get a sense of what each stitch should look like."

She found a pair that satisfied her, and then sat me in the chair behind the cash desk. "Now, do you know how to do a slip knot?"

I could have told her that I'd made grown vampires nearly weep trying to teach me a slip knot, but I merely shook my head. "Right. You can learn that later." And she picked up the wool and needles and made a slip knot in the time it would take me to snap my fingers. "Now, we cast on."

I was clumsy and inept, but I was used to that. However, Eileen was patience personified, and after I'd labored for some time, I had twenty stitches on the needle. "Excellent work," she said, beaming at me, as though I'd presented her with a hand-knit Cashmere pashmina. "Now, we knit the first row."

She showed me how and slowly and painfully, I knit a row. At the end of it, the needles were slick with my sweat and the stitches were a bit wonky, but again, Eileen praised me. "The first row's always the most difficult. The second will be easier."

And it was. Though I felt clumsy, and I was getting a stiff neck from holding myself so tense, as though if I kept perfectly still, I might not drop a stitch. Well, that didn't work, but all I had to do was make a pitiful, panicked sound, and she was ready to show me where I'd gone wrong and then fix it.

She was so comfortable and easy to be around. It was almost like having Gran back.

Customers came and went throughout the morning, some regulars who I could greet by name and to whom I introduced my new assistant, as well as customers who were new to the shop. Eileen insisted I keep knitting and she'd do the serving. "And that way you can let me know if I'm doing it correctly."

I was grunting over my third row, trying not to pull the wool as tight as I usually did, when a woman came in, looking around uncertainly. Eileen went straight up to her and complimented her on her scarf. The woman seemed quite pleased at the compliment and they chatted happily before Eileen asked if she could help her with anything. Before I knew it, the woman was making a sizable purchase of wools and knitting patterns while they chatted away about keeping little boys clean when they insisted on playing outside.

My new assistant didn't have to ask me one question and she rang up the entire purchase and bagged it flawlessly. I complimented her on learning so fast and doing such a great job on her first morning.

She beamed, quite pink with pleasure. "Lucy, dear, it's so kind of you to say so. It does me good to be back in a knitting shop again, dealing with all the delightful people who come in wanting to turn something that was really only sheep's wool not so very long ago into beautiful, wearable art. In our mass-produced world, we don't take enough care of the arts and crafts."

I'd never thought about it that way. In fact, I thought of my shop as a hobby store, but she was right. Keeping alive these traditions was important and perhaps I straightened my shoulders a little and took a bit more pride in my work because of her words.

My mom and dad were working upstairs and had invited a small group of interested students to come by this evening for a meeting. I sent Eileen off for her lunch and when she returned I asked her she'd be comfortable if I left her alone for an hour or so. I had my mobile with me so she could reach me instantly and I promised her I wouldn't go far.

She assured me she'd be fine and so I went upstairs to invite my mother for afternoon tea next door at Elderflower Tea Shop. I'd been too busy to check in on the Miss Watts who ran the tea shop, to see how they were doing since poor Miss Florence Watt's fiancé had been murdered.

I knew Mom would want to see them, as she'd known them since she was a little girl and she was quite happy to take an hour off and join me for afternoon tea. We left my father happily working in front of a computer and headed next door. I'd filled my mother in on the tragedy, already. Sadly, the relationship and subsequent murder had driven a wedge between the two sisters. At one point it had seemed as though they wouldn't be able to continue with the tea shop and I was curious to see how they were getting on.

Miss Mary Watt welcomed us warmly. She was in her early eighties but was as spry and hard-working as a woman much younger. She took both my mother's hands in hers and said, "Why, Susan, it must be five years since I've seen you. Not that you look a day older. I was so sorry about your mother, I miss her every day."

I'd become accustomed to hearing my grandmother spoken of, here in Oxford, but it was still new to my mother. She blinked, rapidly, and then said, "I miss her, too. Especially, now I'm here. It's good to see you, Mary." She glanced around. "And Florence? Is she here?"

Mary's lips thinned, a habit she had when she was perturbed. "Florence is in the kitchen. We're between cooks, at the moment, so she's back to doing the cooking herself, while I run the Tea Shop."

Which meant the sisters rarely had to see each other. It made me sad, as they used to be so close. Mom said that perhaps she'd visit Florence in the kitchen before we left.

Mary seated us at one of the best tables by the window so we could look down on the bustle of Harrington Street. I could keep an eye on my shop next door and, if there was a sudden rush of customers, could easily slip out to help Eileen. However, I didn't expect there'd be a sudden run on wool, and so it turned out. Customers trickled in, and out again, usually with big bags in their hands.

I'd finally hired the perfect assistant, and I felt like I was starting to get the hang of knitting. I felt better about my decision to stay in Oxford than ever before.

Mom looked around and said in a soft voice, "It never changes, does it? I haven't been here for five years and I swear even the flowers on the table are the same."

The flowers were some kind of daisy, mixed with sprigs of lavender. I thought the Watt sisters picked them from their own garden. I knew what Mom meant. From the beamed ceilings, to the lacy cloths and shelves of antique teapots, Elderflower never changed.

Mom said, "I'm so glad you suggested this, Lucy. I haven't had a chance to speak to you alone, not for a minute."

Mom got a certain look in her eye, when we had these one-on-one chats, that made me wary. A bit the way Nyx did if she thought there was a mouse in the vicinity. And like that poor mouse, I felt that one wrong move on my part and I would be pounced upon. I loved my mother, but she sometimes forgot that I'd grown up. When I was with her, I sometimes forgot, too.

"It's great to see you, too, Mom. I'm really glad you came." I wished she hadn't brought a cursed mirror with her, but I didn't bring that up, knowing she didn't remember.

Now that she'd passed the mirror onto me, something about which she had zero recollection, she was perfectly normal. That strange, almost drugged appearance she'd had when she first arrived was gone, and my mother was back. "Honey, we need to talk about your future."

If I had a dollar for every time my mother had said those words I'd have at least a hundred bucks.

I tried to hold onto that feeling I'd had when I first walked in here, that I belonged and was figuring things out. I leaned forward. "Mom, I'm happy here. I don't know if I'll stay forever, but I like running the knitting shop. I like Oxford."

Her forehead creased in a frown. "If only you were clever enough to go to one of the colleges."

Mom was never one to overstate my abilities. I said, "Two intellectuals in the family is probably enough. I know you're disappointed that between you and Dad you didn't pass on the genius gene, but I'm really okay."

"But, darling, you're still so young and the knitting shop seems like something a much older woman should be doing. Have you even learned how to knit?"

That was a sore point. "I'm taking lessons," I assured her. I didn't let on that my teachers were a bunch of very old vampires and a newly-hired shop assistant. I didn't think it was relevant.

"And what about a social life? Have you made any friends? Are you dating?"

I was so happy when Mary Watt came over at that moment and asked us what we wanted to have. We both ordered high tea, with sandwiches, tiny cakes, scones with jam and clotted cream, and a pot of English breakfast tea.

The last time I'd come here for tea, a man had died in front of me. However, it wasn't the fault of the Miss Watts so I tried not to remember that awful day.

People had short memories. Even though two men had

died here, the tea shop was back in operation as though nothing unfortunate had ever taken place.

If anything, business was better. I don't suppose the tourists knew about the tragedy or, perhaps they did, and the tea shop was included in one of those ghost tours of Oxford.

However, my mother was never easily distracted and no sooner had Miss Watt walked away with our order than she turned her laser focused gaze back on me and raised her eyebrows. "Well?"

I reminded myself that I was twenty-seven years old and my mom couldn't make me do anything I didn't want to. Theoretically.

"To answer your questions in order, I do have a social life. I'm starting to make some friends. And, while I'm not exactly dating, I've met a couple of interesting men." Immediately, the images of both Ian Chisholm and Rafe Crosyer rose up in my mind. "I'm not in a rush, Mom. It hasn't been that long since I broke up with The Toad."

She nodded, still looking concerned. "Todd turned out to be a real disappointment. But I hope you won't let his behavior stop you from living a rich and beautiful life."

Why did she think I didn't live a rich and beautiful life, now? Some people would think digging in sand all day, searching out remnants of civilizations that had been dead for thousands of years might not be the most exciting use of a person's time, but did I throw that in my mother's face? No, I did not. Because, it would be impolite. So, why was running a knitting shop in a beautiful city like Oxford not as worthy as digging in sand for dead things? I felt a little irked on behalf of my adopted town.

As though she'd read my mind, Mom said, "It's not that I

don't like Oxford. I was very happy here and, of course, it's where I met your father, when we were both studying. But I know what a pleaser you are, Lucy, and I don't want you to feel obliged to follow your grandmother's wishes." She looked out of the window and tapped her fingertips on the table top. "Not that I would ever speak ill of the dead, especially not my own mother, but your grandmother could be a little high-handed."

I raised my eyebrows at her. "Pot? Kettle?"

She had the grace to laugh. "All right. I appreciate that you want to live your own life. Just make sure it's your life you're living, and not your grandmother's."

"How to make a girl feel really good about herself, Mom. Thanks."

Fortunately, our tea came up at that moment, giving us both a chance to think about something else besides my mother's opinion about my life path. Or lack of one.

Mary was doing all the serving herself, I saw, not that I blamed her. The last time she'd hired help, it hadn't ended so well. But the Watt sisters were not young women and I had to repress the urge to get up and help her.

Mom said, "I wish you could sit and join us for a cup of tea, Mary. I'd love to have a visit with you."

Mary gave her a distracted smile. "There's nothing I'd love more. But I'm a prisoner of this place until we close. The only day we have off is Monday."

"Why don't you both come for dinner? Come tomorrow? We've got nothing on, have we, Lucy?"

Apart from trying to prevent myself from being killed by some ancient monster, no, I didn't have a thing on my agenda. Normally, the vampire knitting club met Thursdays in the shop's back room, but with my parents staying upstairs, and Gran and Sylvia gone, we'd cancelled tomorrow's meeting.

Miss Watt looks quite pleased at the invitation. "I'm certainly available. But it would probably be best if you asked Florence yourself if she's free."

"Of course," said my mother smoothly.

As we poured tea and helped ourselves to tiny salmon, cucumber, and egg sandwiches, Mom said, "It's really sad that those two aren't getting on better. Isn't there something we can do?"

"I honestly don't know. Getting them together over dinner will help. They'll have to be polite in front of us, and, maybe once they start interacting, they'll naturally fall back in into their old ways." I wondered if I might find something in my grimoire that would help. Was there a reconciliation spell?

"Now, what should we give them for dinner?"

I wish she'd thought of that before issuing the dinner invitation. My mother has many wonderful talents—cooking is not one of them. I am more of a throw everything in one pot and hope it turns out, and if it doesn't call for pizza, kind of cook. There wasn't going to be a lot of time for cooking tomorrow, with my mother working on her research projects, and me in the shop all day.

I said, "I'll look on the Internet this afternoon for some simple recipes. We'll think of something." And I could always run down to the pub and get food if we were desperate.

I knew Mom and Dad were here because of that mirror, even if they didn't know it themselves, and, since that witch had said she was drawn to the energy of other witches, and it was my mother who'd unwittingly connected us, I was full of questions.

When we were pleasantly full of little sandwiches, and had moved onto the equally tiny cakes, I said, "Mom, when I was young, did I do anything strange? Inexplicable?" I asked because it seemed so odd that I'd only recently found out I was a witch. I'd had odd feelings and vivid dreams my whole life, but I wondered if Mom had noticed anything extraordinary about me.

Her gaze sharpened on mine and she put her scone back down on her plate in the middle of adding jam to it. "What do you mean? Inexplicable? All children do inexplicable things. They cry for no reason, wake you up in the middle of the night thinking there are monsters under the bed, develop perfectly ridiculous aversions to certain foods. You wouldn't eat broccoli until you were twelve."

She was right, those were the things every kid did. "I meant, did I ever do things that seemed supernatural?"

She sat back and crossed her arms over her chest. Her face was shut down, almost hostile. "Where is this coming from?"

I shrugged, feeling uncomfortable. I couldn't tell her about Gran, or the grimoire, until I was certain she would understand and be sympathetic. And, at the moment, she looked neither understanding nor sympathetic.

"I made your grandmother promise me she wouldn't spout this nonsense to you."

"What nonsense?"

"She was a wonderful woman, your grandmother, and I won't have a word said against her, but she had the oddest notions. Her people came from Ireland, generations ago, you know, and I blame them for filling her head with nonsense. They believed in fairies and selkies and ghosts and I know not what. She had the idea, well, it's ridiculous really, a grown woman, but she had the stubborn notion that we were from a family of witches.

"It's true that one of our ancestors was burned at the stake, but more than likely she was simply a midwife." She stabbed her index finger on the table and looked right into my eyes. "There are no such thing as witches. Your grandmother was filled with superstition, but she was wrong. Your father and I are both scientists, and you must have inherited our rationality."

I was taken aback. I supposed, even as an adult, that I wanted my mother's approval, and her telling me there was no such thing as witches was like someone telling a singer there was no such thing as music.

I was a witch. I knew it. My gran knew it. My cat knew it.

"So, you don't believe in witches?"

"Certainly not."

I pressed on, I don't know why. "Vampires?"

She waved the notion away like a puff of smoke. "Creatures of folklore."

"Ghosts?"

"Children with sheets over their heads at Halloween."

I said, "So, if I told you I was a witch?"

My mother looked seriously worried. If I'd been ten years younger, she'd have leaned across the table and put a hand on my forehead to check for fever. Instead, she said, "I'd suggest therapy. And encourage you to go back home, where your friends are, and where you can live a more rational, orderly life."

I looked out the window and there was Nyx, across the street, staring up at me. She might be staying out of sight now my parents were visiting, but I was comforted, knowing she was keeping an eye on me.

Mom said, "Lucy, I'm thinking about taking a sabbatical next year. You could come back and live with me, maybe go back to school and take a proper degree." I'd managed two years of business college, but never had any desire for a university degree, which was difficult for my extremely educated parents to understand. "You're so young yet, you could do anything you put your mind to."

My mother was already writing grant proposals for funding for the next year. She had this new tomb she'd discovered. I knew perfectly well she'd had no intention of taking a sabbatical; she was offering to give up a year of her career to help me, which I appreciated, but certainly didn't want.

"Thanks, Mom. I'm just asking, hypothetically. I have a customer who comes into the shop. She's a practicing witch. That's why I asked the question." That person was my cousin, Violet Weeks, who was insistent I join her coven for Samhain at the local standing stones, followed by supper.

"Well, don't you fall in with that crowd. Witchcraft is a cult like any other. Stick to the rational, the provable."

I wondered if that was why Mom had no recollection of finding that mirror she'd been impelled to bring it to me. Her mind so rebelled against the possibility of things existing outside the practical, rational world that her mind had shut down rather than accept it.

Which still left me stuck with that mirror and the curse.

CHAPTER 6

For the rest of our tea, we talked about hair. I got my curly hair from my dad. It was all right for him, he could cut his close to the scalp and ignore it. I, on the other hand, was stuck with an unruly mess. If I wanted it to look like I'd spent hours at the salon, I had to spend hours at the salon. Otherwise, I showered and left it to dry and hoped for the best.

Mom had thick, smooth hair, but she bothered even less than I did and it was dry, brittle, and too long. She was trying to decide whether she should change the simple blunt cut she'd had nearly all her life and go for something with a bit more shape to it. "Now that I'm going so gray, I feel like I should put some effort into my hair." It was the first remotely vain statement I'd ever heard my mother make. Suddenly, she leaned forward. "I know. Let's go this very afternoon and get our hair done. Then we can go clothes shopping. It will be such fun, just us girls."

My mother was not the kind of woman who ever said,

'just us girls.' She had to have an ulterior motive. And in a second I knew what it was.

"We've got a few archaeology students coming over tonight," she said, airily. "I hope you don't mind. Of course, Dad and I would love you to meet them and give us your opinion. You're such a good judge of character."

In fact, I'd dated a cheater and been his dupe for two years. That's how good a judge of character I was. But I was not fooled. Mom was hoping I'd fall for one of these archaeology students, and recreate the romance she and my dad had enjoyed. Because it was so sweet of her, and I did need my hair cut, I agreed that a trip to the salon, followed by a bit of shopping, was exactly what I needed.

"I need to run next door and make sure my assistant doesn't need me." In fact, since I was the least competent of the two of us, I felt perfectly happy leaving my shop in Eileen's capable hands.

After we'd all but licked our plates, Mom paid a quick visit to the kitchen to speak to Florence. I declined to visit the kitchen since the last time I'd been in there I'd shared the space with a dead body.

Instead, I talked to Mary Watt. We'd become close when I was involved with the murder that happened in their tea shop and I'd become very fond of the sisters. "It's so nice to see you, Lucy. I wish we saw more of you," Mary said.

"Me, too. But we're both so busy running our businesses."

"I'll look forward to a good catch-up tomorrow." Then she took one of the vases of wild flowers they put on their tables and offered it to me. "I made one too many of our little bouquets. Why don't you have it?"

I thanked her, warmly. They usually put together little bouquets of whatever was growing. Since it was October, there were a couple of orange daisies, a sprig of lavender, and, in this vase, a small branch of rosehips, fat and red. They had dozens of bud vases, but I promised to bring this one back anyway.

Mom returned from the kitchen to say that Florence was delighted to accept our dinner invitation. As we were leaving, I was in front and had my head turned, saying something to my mother, when I physically bumped into someone. I jumped back and so did he and we both laughed at the same time. "Ian. So sorry, I didn't see you." It was Detective Inspector Ian Chisholm, my on again, off again, crush. Today, he looked particularly attractive in a gray overcoat and my crush was instantly on again.

He had his hands on my shoulders where he'd instinctively put them when we crashed. And he left them there for a moment and his blue-green eyes smiled into mine. "Lucy. Nice to see you. I was just bringing some information to Miss Watt."

I nodded. She liked to hear updates of how the case was going against the man who'd murdered her fiancé, and I thought it was real kindness that caused Ian to take time out of his busy schedule to see her.

I introduced my mother, who shook hands with him, and then he went into the tea shop and we proceeded back to my shop. Before we went in, Mom looked at me coyly and asked, "Is he one of those interesting men you were telling me about?"

Trust Mother to ask. I said, "Well, he is interesting."

"Also young and good-looking which a man ought to be if he can possibly manage it."

I laughed. "You sound like a Jane Austen heroine. Anyway, he hasn't even asked me out."

"I'd say, based on the way he looked at you, that he's planning to."

I had the same feeling. And I did everything I could to prevent it happening. It wasn't that I didn't like Ian, I did. And, I was attracted to him. However, my life was complicated enough and the last thing I needed was a police officer finding out the many secrets hidden inside Cardinal Woolsey's.

As I'd guessed, Eileen was perfectly happy to run the shop without me. I was shocked to see how much tidier the place looked since I'd left just over an hour ago. The wools were perfectly stacked within their baskets and on the shelves, and she'd neatened the books and magazines so they all looked untouched. I put the tiny vase of flowers on the immaculate surface of the cash desk and told Eileen of our plan for the afternoon, if she was sure she could manage.

"Oh, yes, dear. You have a lovely time." I gave her my mobile number, in case she needed me, but I doubted very much she'd need to call me.

I introduced Eileen to Mom and they said how happy they were to meet.

"We'll be back by five," Mom told her. Then she explained that there would be four or five students coming, who had expressed an interest in helping with the dig. "I told them to come about five," she said to me. "That's when you close, isn't it?"

"Yes, but tell them to go around to the back and ring up to the flat. Dad can let them in. That way, they don't have to troop through the shop."

Mom looked confused. "It's just so complicated to explain how to get around to the back and down the lane. I find it easier to tell them to come to the shop. You don't mind, do you? Then you can send them straight upstairs."

"Fine."

As we were walking back out the door, Mom said, "I suppose we'll have to give them something to drink and perhaps a snack." She thought for a moment and said, "I'll send your father out."

I knew perfectly well that within five minutes of being upstairs with prospective students, both of them would be so immersed in talking shop they'd forget all about snacks, and all other practical matters. "I'll get them," I said.

When we left, Mom and I headed toward Cornmarket Street. "I should have made a salon appointment," I said, realizing that getting two of us into a salon was going to be touch and go.

She giggled, a girlish sound very unlike my mother. "I took the liberty of making appointments for us when you came up to invite me for tea. I was sure that if you could take time out for afternoon tea, you could manage a salon visit."

"That's great, Mom." I was pleased she'd taken the initiative. Even if she did have an ulterior motive, trying to set me up with an archaeology student, I was happy to spend an afternoon with my mom. Who knew how many more I had?

As we walked down Cornmarket, I noticed how many stores had Halloween displays. Halloween never used to be a UK tradition, but, like so many things, it's an American celebration that's become popular. Little kids dressed as goblins, going door to door to collect candy, what's not to like?

Of course, for the witches among us, Halloween was the

day before Samhain, one of the eight most important Wiccan holidays. My cousin, Violet Weeks, had been pestering me to come to her coven's Samhain event, at the standing stones near Moreton-Under-Wychwood. I'd said I'd think about it, but if the demon hadn't got me by then, I thought I'd go, and see if I could get some ideas in how to vanquish a very ancient and powerful dark wizard. And, as a side note, I'd really like to free Meritamun from her mirrored prison.

The day was cold and overcast, but Cornmarket was still thronged with tourists, students, and regular people who lived here. Oh, and a couple of vampires, I noted, catching sight of Rafe and Clara, walking in the same direction. They looked a bit like a son taking his mother out for the afternoon. And the way she looked up at him, hanging on his every word, she looked every inch the proud mother.

I was happy to have my undead protectors and enjoyed the way they managed to keep me and Mom under surveillance, without ever seeming to glance our way.

We got to the corner of Queens and Cornmarket and there was a tour group standing at the base of Carfax Tower looking up at the little figures around the clock that would come out when the clock chimed.

"Terrible waste," Mom remarked as we walked past. "That was a medieval church, you know. And they knocked it down in Victorian times to make room for the traffic." Mom's not a fan of knocking old things down to make way for the new.

"I know. But at least most of the historic buildings are protected now," I said, going for the positive.

We walked on, toward Oxford Castle, which had some of the city's old Saxon walls on display. However, we weren't getting our hair done in the old prison, I was happy to see.

Instead, she turned down a side street I didn't know, and led us to a salon tucked away in the old industrial section, where the breweries used to be.

The salon featured brick walls, an offer of cappuccino when we walked in, and stylists who looked as though they knew what they were doing. They seated us side by side and Mom explained to her stylist that she wanted something easy to care for, but more stylish.

My stylist, a woman about my own age, with stick straight hair, lifted a handful of my curls and said, "What are we doing today?"

My hair is what it is. If I keep it long, it doesn't frizz so badly, but it requires more time than I can give it to look stylish. Mostly, I keep it trimmed and use enough product to tame the curl. When I explained all this, the stylist nodded and said, "I'll trim the ends and see what we can do about taming the beast."

I nodded. "Sounds good." I felt as though cold fingers were walking up my neck and glanced out the window to see Rafe and Clara gazing in the window. I felt safer knowing they were watching out for me.

When we'd finished our hair, Mom looked about ten years younger. Her hair was softer around her face and they'd done a moisturizing treatment so it looked thicker and more healthy. Since we were in the neighborhood, I took her to Westgate Shopping Center, a modern, American-style mall on three levels.

Her eyes opened wide when she saw it. "This wasn't here five years ago," she exclaimed.

Most of the high street shops were represented, as were a lot of international stores. Mom stocked up on cotton trousers and shirts suitable for digging up skeletons in the desert, then I told her she had to buy something pretty. I talked her into going into the Ted Baker store where she tried on several dresses.

"When would I ever wear this?" she asked, modeling a navy, floral dress that looked stunning on her.

"When Dad takes you out for dinner in Oxford," I said. "It will be good for you two to have a real date."

"I haven't splurged like this for so long," she said, and then, with a sudden nod, said, "I'll take it."

As we left, she insisted we walk through the John Lewis department store and see if there was something for me. I didn't really need anything, either, but, with the help of a very helpful shop assistant, I ended up trying on three dresses.

The first was dark blue with flowers patterned on it. Mom liked it. I glanced behind me, to where Rafe and Clara were pretending to browse. Clara nodded and smiled, but Rafe shook his head.

The second dress was green, with a low-cut neckline and a full skirt. Mom said, "Honey, that looks fantastic. Clara gave another nod and a smile. I thought I could try on every dress in the mall and get approval from Clara, but Rafe shook his head.

I put the third dress on. It was black. Simply cut, but figure hugging. I could imagine walking down the streets of Paris in this one. I walked out and my gaze went straight to Rafe's. He took in the outfit and nodded, once.

Mom and I walked back to Cardinal Woolsey's, bags hanging from our wrists, like a couple of normal shoppers. Who'd have known one of us had a death curse hanging over her?

At least, if I was going to die, I'd look good.

Mom went around the back to the main entrance of the flat, taking my shopping bags with her, and I walked into the front door of Cardinal Woolsey's.

Eileen was standing on a chair dusting the corners of the ceiling. I felt immediately guilty. I'd been out shopping and my underpaid assistant was all but scrubbing the floors. "You don't have to do the cleaning."

She turned and smiled down at me. "Cleanliness is next to godliness, dear."

She didn't say it like criticism, but I silently promised to keep a better handle on the dusting and sweeping so this much older woman didn't end up climbing on chairs and doing it herself.

I noticed that everything was just that much more orderly. The baskets never quite lined up, and yet, somehow Eileen had got them to sit in perfect rows.

"Did you have any customers?"

"A few. There was a lovely young woman who is expecting twins. She came with her mother who's going to knit layettes for both babies. We had such fun looking at the little booties and bonnets, it took me back to when my children were babies. That was quite a nice sale," she said, sounding satisfied.

I checked back on the cash register and my eyes widened. The expectant mom and grandma had spent more than two hundred pounds. I was delighted.

Since my shop was running so well, and there was currently no customer needing me, I opened my computer and began searching for simple dinner recipes. While I was out getting the snacks tonight I might as well get the ingredients for dinner tomorrow.

"Chicken Cordon Bleu?" I mused aloud. I didn't really fancy stuffing and rolling chicken breasts. "Beef Wellington?" I could buy that already done at the butcher in the covered market and then all I'd have to do would be roast potatoes and vegetables. It seemed rather a heavy dish, though.

"Trying to choose a recipe?" Eileen asked.

I explained my dilemma, that my mom had invited the ladies next door, who were in their eighties, to dinner. None of us had time to cook properly and besides I admitted neither my mom, nor I, nor my dad were particularly good cooks.

Eileen said, "Would you let me cook for you? I love to cook and now that my dear husband has passed away, and my children are grown up with their own families, I have no one to cook for. I'd be pleased to do it as a thank you to you for giving me this job, which I already love."

"Not as much as I love having you here," I said, with heartfelt sincerity.

"I make an excellent shepherd's pie, if I might suggest that. It's already got the potatoes and the vegetables in it, of course. It's also very easy to eat, if they have false teeth. And I can do a sherry trifle for dessert—a little old-fashioned, I know, but, again, older people appreciate the more traditional desserts. What do you think?"

I thought I'd fallen asleep and dreamed this magical fairy into my life, is what I thought. Shepherd's pie just happened to be one of my favorite dishes. And my dad had fallen in love with trifle when he was a student here at Oxford. Still, I hesitated. "Eileen, I can't let you do this. It's such a lot of work and you just started this full-time job."

"Nonsense. I've got a great deal of energy, and I shall enjoy it. Now, I don't want to hear anymore nonsense from you, young lady."

I smiled and thanked her and insisted on giving her the money to go shopping before she left, instead of settling up afterwards, as she'd suggested. I thought, perhaps, I could give her some extra time off at some later date to make up for the time she'd no doubt spend cooking dinner for people she didn't even know.

CHAPTER 7

*J*ust before five, Mom wandered into the shop, looking slightly vague. She had her reading glasses on, which didn't help. She said, "Lucy, I'm not sure you have enough chairs."

Since I was in the middle of counting skeins of superwash worsted, it took me a moment to register what she was talking about. "Chairs?"

"Yes, for our meeting, tonight. I just counted the chairs upstairs and I don't think there are enough. Some of the grad students might have to sit on the floor."

"Are these the same grad students who are going to spend the summer living in tents and shoveling sand all day, uncovering ancient ruins? Do you really think they're going to mind sitting on the floor?"

"Sweetheart, we don't want to give them the wrong impression."

I didn't intend to run out and buy or rent more chairs, so I said, "Why don't you use the back room of the shop, where we run the knitting classes? I've got enough chairs there for twenty people."

She smiled at me. Blinking owlishly. "I knew you'd have the answer. You're so good at practical things. And don't forget the pizza."

I had no idea what she was talking about, but after nearly three decades with my parents, I was pretty good at filling in the blanks. "You want me to order enough pizza for everybody who's coming tonight. And how many is that?"

"Not more than a dozen, I shouldn't think. I told them to come at five."

Eileen paused in putting together sweater kits and said, "Dr. Bartlett-Swift, you have a lovely daughter, and she runs an excellent shop. All her clients rave about her."

I was certain that couldn't be true. I think most of my clients were horrified that I knew so little about knitting, wool, and pretty much everything to do with the knitting shop. But it was sweet of Eileen to say those nice things, especially when Mom had been questioning my decision to stay in Oxford and run Cardinal Woolsey's.

My mother blinked and then finally pulled her glasses up to the top of her head so she could see clearly. "Not to be outdone, she said, "Lucy was telling me what an excellent help you've been to her, and on your first day, too. She's so pleased she hired you."

Having complimented each other to their mutual satisfaction, the two ladies returned to what they were previously doing. Eileen back to preparing kits to make sweaters, and mother back upstairs, no doubt to her computer.

I was about to pick up the phone and order pizza to be delivered about six, but then one of my regular customers came in. She was a new mother. The woman had been a professional banker who traveled all over Europe and managed an international staff, but managing one baby was, she said, the most difficult job she'd ever done. Knitting had saved her sanity.

"I'm making Christmas presents for everyone, this year," she announced. She looked slightly wild-eyed and I think there was baby spit up in her hair. The baby was currently asleep in its pram but I knew from experience that it would wake, and would emit a tremendous amount of noise for such a small human.

"Are you sure," I asked. "It's only two months until Christmas, and with the baby..." I let her fill in the rest of the sentence with whatever the baby did that kept her from having showers.

"Yes. I'm too Type A not to juggle projects." She looked at me the way a chocoholic eyes a box of perfect truffles. "I need this."

At that very moment, ominous sounds came from the pram. One of the reasons this woman came to my shop was the gift I have with babies. Sure enough, when I walked toward the pram and said, "May I?" she nodded with true gratitude. "Would you?"

I picked up the little boy before he'd gone from mildly unhappy to nuclear meltdown and, after some half-hearted sobs, he curled against me, his tiny fingers clutching my sweater.

I began to rock him and speak softly, as our breathing synchronized and he drifted back to sleep. "She has a real gift," his mother said to Eileen.

I had a sneaking suspicion I'd been using magic on kids

without ever realising it. Keeping my voice low, I said, "Do you have any particular gifts in mind?"

"Let me, Lucy," Eileen said, coming forward. "I was looking at this Christmas knitting magazine that only came in today. There are projects for every member of the family, and some are quite easy." She led the banker over to the magazines and left me, contentedly rocking.

It was so nice, and peaceful, that I was able to forget about my own threatened death for a while, and enjoy this tiny bundle of warm, breathing life.

I was hoping to skip Mom and Dad's meeting, here in the shop, and go upstairs to work in secret with my grimoire. I didn't like the feeling of impending doom that had hovered about me, ever since that woman had spoken to me from the other side of the mirror. Being cursed with probable death was messing with my life plans.

We were surprisingly busy the last hour. I think a tour bus must've come in from an area with no knitting shops, for a number of ladies with similar northern accents came in and took over the shop. I heard one of them say to Eileen, "We've nothing as nice as this at home."

"I'll be bound you don't," said Eileen, pouncing on the ladies the way a hungry cat might pounce on some very fat, delicious looking mice. I helped serve them, but Eileen was much better at moving the merchandise than I was. I wondered how I'd managed without her. I was even adding some inventory items that Eileen had recommended. It was only her first day and she'd already improved my business no end.

The door opened again, nearly at closing time and, since Eileen was busy with the last of her juicy mice, I glanced up, ready to say, "Can I help you?" only to see it was the sun-streaked hottie from this morning.

He grinned his I-could-eat-you-all-up grin and said, "G'day. How you goin'?"

"I'm fine." I glanced at my watch. "You're a little early."

He came closer and leaned a hip against my cash desk. "Well, it's like this. I had fifteen minutes to spare. I could've dropped into the pub at the end of the road and had a beer, but the trouble with one beer is it always leads to another beer, then I'd miss the meeting." He put his hands up in a helpless fashion. "I reckoned I could come and spend a little time with you before we started."

I shook my head at him. He was too smooth for his own good. Still, I was happy I'd had my hair done, and I may have tossed it over my shoulder. I was a female, after all. "As flattered as I am, I'm working until five. You're welcome to go on into the back room, though, that's where the meeting will be. I'll tell my parents you're here."

"No worries," he said. "Have you got Wi-Fi? I can check my emails."

I gave him the Wi-Fi password and off he went into the back room.

The last of the ladies left, hurrying to catch their coach. Very soon, my sharp ears picked up noises coming from the back room, noises that I did not like at all. In fact, I didn't like anyone being there without my supervision, because of the trapdoor that leads down into the tunnels beneath Oxford, where my grandmother and her friends have their home. I kept it locked from my side, when I didn't want vampire visitors coming up, but it was a simple enough thing to open when you were on this side of it.

Eileen had just ushered her happy customers out of the door, so I fought the urge to run to the back room and make an issue of it.

I waited a moment and then I said, as casually as I could, "I'll just check that he's got everything." I pulled aside the curtain into the back room and, to my horror, found my Australian friend on his hands and knees about to lift up the trapdoor. Before I could think of modulating my voice, I shrieked," What do you think you're doing?"

He turned to look at me over his shoulder, still on his hands and knees, looking unabashed, and grinned. "I'm an archaeologist. We're always digging to find what's underneath things. I had a bit of trouble with the latch, but I've got it, now."

I went over and very firmly stood in the middle of the trapdoor, my boot tips an inch from his fingers. "There's nothing down there but sewers. And rats. I never open this door, as I don't want disgusting smells and even more disgusting vermin up here. I'd appreciate it if you'd leave that alone." My heart was pounding and I felt hot and flustered. Also angry with myself for letting anyone back here unsupervised.

He got up, slowly, and dusted his hands off. Behind me I heard Eileen say, "Well, I never."

I turned to her and asked, "What happened to the rug that always sits over this door?" I kept it there for a reason.

Her pink lips formed an O. "It was so dusty, I took it outside to beat it with a broom and I thought I'd just let it hang outside for couple of hours to air out. It's in your back garden. I'm so sorry, I'll go and get it, right away."

I appreciated that she was being extra zealous on her first

day, but still, I shuddered to think what could have happened if the Australian student had found his way down into the tunnels and bumped into one of the vampires.

He said, "I've always wanted to go down there. There are many entrances, you know. T.E. Lawrence famously rowed a boat through those tunnels. I think it was a kayak. Or maybe it was a canoe. You know, Lawrence of Arabia."

"Yes, I know. It's not a river down there, now, if it ever was. It's sewers. Trust me, you do not want to be down there, in a canoe or anything else."

I wasn't certain if he believed me, but I'm fairly certain he got the message that if he wanted to explore subterranean Oxford, then he was going to have to find another entrance than the one from my shop. I knew there were lots; it was how the vampires moved around the city on sunny days or if they just wanted to stay out of sight.

Eileen brought the rug back in and, with further apologies, laid it on top of the trapdoor. I wasn't about to leave the Aussie un-chaperoned, so I said, "What's your name? And whereabouts are you in your studies?"

"My name's Pete. Pete Taylor. I did my first degree in Sydney, in geology but I came to Oxford because I want to learn about stratigraphy—that's analyzing the layer and order of geological strata when we document finds. I'm studying the proper techniques for survey, interpreting, and recording finds. Which your parents are famous for. I mean, doing it right on site. I love to dig down and see something no human eye has looked on for hundreds or even thousands of years. It's such a rush."

"To each his own, I guess. I've been on digs with my parents when all I remember is the heat, the bugs, and the sand. One summer it seemed like everything I ate was crunchy."

Eileen's voice interrupted us. "And here are your next two guests."

Another guy about my age, with curly hair, thick glasses, and a scholarly look to him arrived with a woman I'd have put in her thirties. Her black hair was tied back and she was wearing jeans and a plaid shirt. I'd met so many students like these two when they'd been working with my parents. I'd had crushes on a couple of the better looking guys who, of course, never paid any attention to me.

The guy with the glasses introduced himself as Logan Douglas and, as he and Pete shook hands, he said, "I know you from somewhere."

Pete looked surprised, then shook his head. "You've probably seen me in one of the pubs." He winked at me. "It happens."

Logan pushed up his glasses. "No. It was at Glastonbury. I'm sure of it."

Pete clapped him on the shoulder, in a man-to-man way. "Right, the musical festival, that was it. Good memory."

I could tell the other guy was about to say something else, but Pete leaned past him to the young woman and introduced himself to her. Her name was Priya Sandeep. She was studying to be a ceramicist, someone who spends their entire life looking at ancient tiles. It's incredible the way some people want to spend their lives. And Mom thought I was throwing myself away on a knitting shop?

I realized Eileen was still standing there. No doubt she was waiting for permission to leave. I walked out with her into the main shop. I could barely find the words to express how grateful I was. "Thank you so much for your help, today, Eileen. I don't know what I would've done without you."

"It's been a pleasure." She hesitated, and then said, "My bus gets here half an hour before the shop opens. This morning I went and had a coffee, but I'd just as soon come in a bit early and get things ready. If that's all right with you."

"Yes, of course." Mornings were hectic, with my parents staying here, and I'd barely made it downstairs in time to prepare the shop for opening. I said, "I'll give you a key. Then you can let yourself in, whenever you need to."

I got the extra key out of the drawer, and gave it to her.

"Lovely," she said. "See you tomorrow."

As she left, two more grad students arrived and I sent them into the back room and then ran upstairs to remind my mother and father that the meeting they had arranged was about to begin. They were both deeply immersed in work. My father was typing away on his computer and my mother appeared to be researching something on hers.

Both looked up at me as though I might be speaking a language other than English, and then, as my words sank in, they said in unison, "Ah. The meeting."

My dad said, "Are the students here, already?"

"Yes."

My mother said, "How many turned up?"

"There are five down there now and I have no idea how many there will be altogether."

"We'll come down," said my dad, though he looked at his screen as though sad to part with it.

I went down with them and, while they went into the back room, to explain about the project to the interested post grads, I phoned for pizza. They had no delivery person, tonight, the woman on the phone explained, but, if I could come and pick them up, they would have my pizzas ready in thirty minutes.

I walked up to get the pizzas and, dodging a crowd of young men who were celebrating some kind of sports win, I headed to The Golden Cross, off Cornmarket, where there's a Pizza Express tucked into a twelfth century building. There are medieval wall paintings which you can look at while munching your marinara.

A shadow appeared beside me and I jumped. "You scared me," I said to Rafe, as he fell into step beside me.

"You asked me to meet you. I can show you the text," he said, as though I might have forgotten I texted him.

"I know, but even when I'm expecting you, you appear out of thin air."

He looked amused. "That's a talent your people have, not mine."

"Whatever." I couldn't imagine ever being able to disappear and reappear, but then I was basically at the level of Witching 101. "I need your help figuring out this mirror."

He said, "I've been doing some research, and there is reference to a cult of dark and powerful creatures who kill off white witches."

"Is this creature a dark witch?"

"More a demon, I think. A stealer of souls. He's Egyptian in origin, but was certainly active and known to be in Salem during the witch trials. And was also likely here in the UK on witch hunts. He can take many disguises and no one, yet, has been able to stop or destroy him."

"And this is the dude who's after me?" I glanced up and down the crowded street, wondering if that guy selling magazines might be after my soul. Or could it be that homeless man, sitting on an old blanket, reading. Or maybe his dog, curled up beside him.

"I wish I had better news," Rafe said, sounding worried.

"The girl in the mirror said he trapped her. She's got some kind of power where she can reach out to other witches, and somehow she latched onto me."

He had a true scholar's way of looking at things. "That's interesting. I wonder if it's because you've recently discovered your own powers and that triggered her awareness of you. A little like a diver who cuts themselves and then the sharks scent the blood. They coexisted peacefully in the ocean until the blood spilled and then the hunt was on."

"Great analogy. Very comforting. Thanks."

"Lucy, sarcasm won't save you."

I turned to him. "What will save me? That's the real question, here."

"I'm working on that."

"I'd feel a whole lot better if you didn't sound so worried when you said that." We passed a young couple, holding hands, clearly students. I waited until they were out of earshot. "What I need is a super witch. Someone older, with more power, who might have some idea how to help me fight this thing."

He looked down at me. "I might know someone."

"But? The way you said that there was an implied but."

"You've been hidden until now, incognito if you will. Once

you enter this powerful witch's circle, you'll forever be part of it."

A shiver went over my skin. I felt like I was being given a choice. I could be killed by some horrible soul-sucking demon, probably in some very unpleasant way, or I could be drawn into a powerful witch's coven. I'd been able to avoid joining my cousin's circle, I wasn't sure I'd fare as well with a more powerful witch. I wished there was a third option. And maybe there was.

"What if I could free that girl? She's clearly a witch, too, and nobody knows his power like she does. What if I could somehow break the spell that binds her?"

"That's an excellent idea. How will you free her?"

Here we came to the sticking point of my great plan. "I don't know."

He turned to me, as dark and mysterious as the ancient city at his back. "Have you even been practicing your magic?"

"Yes." I sounded defensive even to my own ears. "But I'm busy with the shop and my life."

"Well, if we want that life to continue, we're going to have to figure out a way to stop this creature."

I felt much better now that he was using 'we.' Rafe might not be a witch, but he was a very powerful vampire. I was certain he could help me if he put his mind to it.

"I want you to keep yourself safe. Try not to be alone. How's your new assistant working out so far?"

I thought of comfortable, safe. Eileen Percival had had one more reason to be glad I'd hired her. "She's the perfect assistant. I feel completely safe with her."

"Good. With customers coming and going, plus your assistant, you should be safe enough during shop hours." He held up a finger in warning. "Don't do this again, coming out in the evening, alone. Especially not going down deserted side streets."

"I knew I was meeting you."

"Yes, but when I appeared, you jumped like a frightened rabbit. You didn't take any defensive action."

Damn. I was really going to have to up my game. "I keep forgetting I'm a witch."

"Well, the demon isn't forgetting, so I suggest you don't, either." He sounded stern, and I knew it was because he was worried about me.

I said, "I'll try and talk to the girl in the mirror again tonight. She seems to appear whenever I recite the spell. I'll ask her if the mirror can be destroyed. She's on the inside of it, with plenty of time to think. She must have some ideas." I gnawed my lip. "And, I'd better meet your super witch."

"I think that's wise."

He slipped back into the shadows while I went into the restaurant and picked up the pizzas. Rafe carried them as we walked home, and when we passed a Tesco Express convenience store, I said I'd better go in and get some soft drinks.

"You have plates and napkins?" Rafe asked.

"No. Thanks for reminding me. How is it you know everything?"

"When you've been around as long as I have, you learn a thing or two."

I picked up some bottles of sparkling water and juices as well as napkins and paper plates, and we carried the lot back to my shop.

Rafe slipped away and I walked in, where Dad was in full lecture mode. Six prospective students sat in a rough oval, with Mom and Dad at one skinny end of the oval. The students all had notebooks out and looked keen.

As I put the pizzas and things on the table, as quietly as I could, Pete looked up and winked at me. I gave him a little wave. Then, feeling certain that I wouldn't be needed, I slipped upstairs.

Nyx followed me. She seemed to spend her time wherever my parents weren't, and she'd stopped even posing in my front window. Now, she was out most of the time. I thought that magic mirror was freaking her out, and I didn't blame her. Still, I missed her warm comfort and was happy she'd decided to come inside for a while. As soon as we arrived upstairs, I fed her a can of tuna and freshened her water.

I ought to eat, too, but I was too wound up. She followed me upstairs into my bedroom. I shut the door and retrieved the leather bag containing the mirror from where I'd hidden it in my bedside drawer, behind a novel. On top of it I'd piled a flashlight I kept there in case the lights went out, pen and paper, and a packet of tissues. Nyx eyed the bag warily and, when I pulled out the mirror, she arched her back and hissed and then jumped onto the windowsill and shot out the window.

I'd left the window open only about an inch, but she was so anxious to be out, she squeezed her body through the opening, flattening herself like a cat-shaped tube of toothpaste. She obviously sensed that there was nothing good about this mirror. I wished I could run away from it. I didn't want to be anywhere near this thing, either. I had a very strong feeling that this wasn't something I could run away from. This was going to be one of those challenges I had to face head-on.

I took a deep breath and tried to center myself, but my heart was beating so fast I was breathless. I recited the incantation on the mirror. As before, the blue light began to radiate and the young girl appeared in the wavy surface of the mirror, like an apparition on top of the sea.

"You are still alive," she said, sounding amazed.

"Yes. And I plan to stay that way for as long as possible. Meritamun, you've been inside that mirror for a long time. Do you think it can be destroyed?"

She said, "I think it may be possible. It would take a very hot fire and the correct spell." She looked very sad as she said the words, but she raised her chin in what looked like bravado.

"Meritamun, if I destroy the mirror, what will happen to you?"

"I will suffer the same fate."

I was filled with horror. "You mean, if I'm able to destroy this mirror, perhaps by burning it and melting the bronze, you would burn up with it?"

She nodded. And a single tear tracked down her cheek. "Do not hesitate. It is my fate. I have been an instrument of evil, it is only right that I should perish."

"But that wasn't your fault. You're an unwilling victim of evil. No, there has to be another way."

She said, "I do not know what it is. Better I should be destroyed than to continue to bring death to my people."

She began to fade. "But, wait, there must be some other way. Can't we break the original spell? The one that trapped you?"

"To destroy the evil spell, you would have to destroy my

master." At least, I thought that's what she said, she faded away on the last words.

I felt as though I were playing a bit part in a horror movie. Evil warlocks and trapped maidens? Seriously? And, like the bit player in the movie, I wasn't powerful enough to fight any of them. I was seriously worried that in this movie, I was that girl who hears the noise in the basement, and goes to see what it is, in her nightgown. I was even blonde.

Not only did I not want to die some horrific death, I didn't want to leave that poor girl cursed any longer, either.

I retrieved my family's spell book from where I kept it hidden, at the back of my closet. Okay, it wasn't a great hiding place, but the book was spellbound so anyone who stole it would have to break a powerful spell to gain access. I opened the book and searched for spells that would release a trapped witch.

There was an interesting story, handwritten in faded ink, about a witch who'd been trapped in a bottle in the 1800s. That seemed close enough to being trapped in a mirror, that I wondered if I could release the witch using the same method. I eagerly read the piece and discovered the bottle containing the witch was on display at the Pitt Rivers Museum, right here in Oxford. A note in my grandmother's hand said, "Presumably, the poor witch is still trapped inside."

Well, and wasn't that just great? If the local witches couldn't release their old friend, what chance did I have of springing a witch from a three-thousand–year-old mirror?

Rafe was right. I was going to have to visit his friend, the super witch.

I texted Rafe and said I would like him to introduce me to

his friend as soon as possible. He texted back with one word. Understood.

A little later he texted back. Dawn tomorrow and an address. I Googled the address and it was a good ten miles out of town, in a place called Moreton-Under-Wychwood, which sounded like a charming English village. But I knew of this place. It was where my witch cousin, Violet Weeks, and her grandmother, Lavinia lived. I was going to have to visit witch central. At dawn.

I thumbed through my grimoire, now looking for a spell that would protect me from harm. Whoever had put this grimoire together was no archivist. It was a mess of spells and stories, with no rhyme or reason. No wonder I wasn't learning anything. I felt like someone had told me to learn Latin and then chucked the complete works of Virgil and Horace at me. I didn't know where to start.

I was not looking forward to driving Gran's old car to this witch's house ten miles away, at dawn. I hated driving in the UK. I could never get on with the other side of the road business.

While I was fretting, I got another text. Rafe again. He told me he would pick me up in his car at six in the morning. I may not have loved how high-handed he was, but I could forgive a lot to a man who was willing to chauffeur me before the crack of dawn.

One good thing about leaving the house so early was that I wouldn't have to explain my actions to my parents, who would hopefully sleep through my whole encounter with the super witch.

I only wished I could.

CHAPTER 8

I went to bed early, but of course, I couldn't sleep. My dreams were troubled by visions of fire and death and a dark shadowy creature who could have been a figment of my imagination, but I knew from the sense of dread that this was the evil demon.

When my alarm woke me at five, I was completely stunned. It took me a moment to realize why my eyes were awake in the pitch dark. I flipped on the light and found that Nyx had come in sometime in the night and was curled beside me. I patted her for a little bit and then told her to go back to sleep.

She didn't, though, she watched me through slitted green eyes as I dressed in black jeans and a loose fitting black linen shirt. I slipped on dark socks and then black ankle boots wondering why I felt the need to dress all in black just because I was going to visit a witch. If I'd had a pointy hat I'd have probably put that on, too, and if I could ride a broom that would've come in handy.

I slipped on the red shawl Theodore had made me, almost defiantly. Then I crept downstairs and made coffee. Strong coffee. I might have to meet a scary witch, but I wasn't doing it without a lot of caffeine in my system.

As I went to let myself out of the house, I realized Nyx was following me.

"No, Nyx," I whispered, not wanting to take her to a place I didn't want to go myself. She slid along behind me, like a low, creeping shadow. Finally, I pulled the mirror out of my bag and the cat shrank away. As I crept out of the flat I could hear my dad snoring.

When I got to our meeting spot, in the back lane, Rafe was already there in his sleek, black Tesla. I slipped into the passenger seat, did up my seatbelt and he took off almost immediately. He glanced at me. "Nervous?"

He, of course, was wide-awake. I, on the other hand, was groggy and tired after a restless night plagued with bad dreams. Not too tired to be nervous, however, and I nodded briefly.

"Don't let her intimidate you," was his advice. Great, really helpful. That made me much less nervous.

"Who is this super-witch?" I asked.

"Margaret Twig is her name. She was born in Ontario, in Canada. Her father was a botanist, I believe, and the family lived in the wilderness where he did his studies and wrote books. He taught her about plants, and her mother taught her about natural remedies, much of it gleaned from the aboriginal people of the area."

"She's a fellow North American, then."

"Yes. But, she's been here for decades. She came to the UK

to study natural medicine and connect with her mother's people."

"The witches in the family."

"That's right. She's the unofficial leader of the Oxford-shire witches."

Driving ten miles before dawn, even on tiny country roads near Oxford, didn't take us very long. The lights of the silent car illuminated the twisting road ahead and dark masses of trees that must be the remains of the original Wychwood forest. Overhead the trees met in a canopy so it was like driving in a dark tunnel.

Rafe drove as though he knew these roads intimately, which I expect he did. His home was out this way. My geography was a bit vague, especially in the dark, but his home was near Woodstock and we'd passed through that village. We were in country, now, with few lights showing in the scattered farmhouses. A wooden signpost pointed to Shipton-Under-Wychwood, so I knew we were getting close to Moreton-Under-Wychwood, where my mother's side of the family came from, and where the witch, Margaret Twig, lived.

Pink and purple light was beginning to streak the sky when we arrived at a low Cotswold stone cottage that sat by itself in a large field. A curl of smoke rose from the chimney. I got out of the car, clutching the leather bag containing the mirror, and Rafe came around the car and, to my surprise, took my hand in his. Even though his hand was cool, it was a very comforting gesture. I felt better knowing he was with me.

We trod up a stone path and up two stone steps. There was a black, wrought iron door knocker, shaped like a pixie, on an ancient oak door. Rafe wrapped smartly on the door and soon a woman opened it.

"Good morning," she said. "I'm Margaret Twig. You must be Lucy?" I agreed that I was and she motioned us to come inside. She and Rafe did the French double-cheek kissing thing.

Margaret Twig was a confusing mix of the eccentric and the sophisticated. She was short and wiry with gray hair that sprang out in corkscrew curls all over her head, bright blue eyes that tilted up the corners like a cat's, a sharp nose, a very definite chin.

"You found the place all right in the dark?" Her voice was low and quick, with a flat North American accent.

"No trouble at all," Rafe answered.

She wore a turquoise flowered one-piece jumpsuit that would've looked more at home in Hawaii or the Caribbean than the English countryside. Around her neck she wore a quantity of colorful beads. I found her fascinating and definitely intimidating.

The lights were on and she led us down a flagstone corridor. The ceilings were beamed with dark wood and so low that Rafe had to duck through the doorways. We entered a large kitchen at the back of the house. The kitchen was a blend of new and old. An Aga stove against one wall, sending a comforting warmth into the air. Against the opposite wall was an Inglenook fireplace, the perfect size to roast an ox, and hanging from it, were various cast-iron implements.

Suspended in the center was a large, black cauldron. Hanging at the side of the fireplace was a whisk broom that looked ready to take off and fly. In a decorating magazine the cast iron pots would look stylish, in keeping with the age of the cottage. But I suspected they saw regular use.

She caught me staring and I asked, stupidly, "Is that a cauldron?"

Her eyes twinkled in a disturbing way, as though she were laughing at me. "Yes, it is." She pointed to an open pantry lined with jars of herbs. "I keep the eye-of-newt and bats' wings in the pantry."

I blinked at her in shock, and she turned to Rafe. "Doesn't have much sense of humor, does she?"

He said, "Be nice, Margaret. Lucy's trying to break a curse."

She rubbed her hands together, looking quite pleased. "Yes, let's see this spellbound object I've been hearing about."

I drew out the mirror and handed it to her. She walked into the kitchen and took a pair of tortoiseshell-framed glasses from a shelf and put them on. She studied the mirror under the full glare of the kitchen light.

"This is beautiful," she said. "How old did you say it was, Rafe?"

"About 1500 BCE. Lovely, isn't it?"

I felt like we were in the middle of an episode of Antiques Roadshow and they were about to tell me what I could get for the mirror at auction. I said, somewhat sharply, "It's also cursed and apparently, now that I'm in possession of this thing, some horrible demon is going to come and kill me."

"Mmm," said Margaret, "That does lessen its value a bit."

I could not believe she was joking about this. Rafe said, "Can you read ancient Egyptian?"

She shook her head. He said, "Lucy, give her the words of

the incantation while she's holding the mirror, and let her recite them herself."

"Why?"

"I'm curious to see whether, in the hands of another witch, the incantation will activate the magic." To Margaret he said, "When I recited the words, while holding the mirror, nothing happened. But every time Lucy says them...well, you'll see."

I had to give Margaret credit, she showed absolutely no hesitation about possibly calling forth a death curse. She held onto the mirror's handle quite firmly and said, "Give me the words and I'll repeat them. I walked over and stood behind her, but not so close any part of me was reflected.

Even though I knew the incantation by heart, by now, I didn't want to make even the slightest error. I gave her the words, phrase by phrase, and she repeated them. When she got to the last word I think we all held our breath.

Nothing happened.

"Interesting," Margaret said. "It doesn't curse any witch who touches it, only, presumably, the one it was intended for."

Rafe was leaning against the granite countertop, watching us. "Have you seen such a spell before?"

"I don't want to comment until I've seen it in action." She handed the mirror to me. "Lucy? Would you?"

I had the most ridiculous fear that now we'd come out here, I'd read the words and nothing would happen, and I'd look foolish in front of this eccentric, but rather marvelous, woman. Which was absurd, because the best thing that could happen to me would be to find the curse had fizzled out or moved on, or been a figment of my imagination the whole time.

I took a breath and, before I could speak, Margaret touched my shoulder. When I glanced up, she looked deep into my eyes and held my gaze. "Center yourself. I can feel your nerves jangling so loud they sound like wind chimes in a storm. Don't let your fear show, or the powers of evil will use it against you."

I swallowed and nodded, trying to tame my fear.

"That's right," she said in that low, flat voice. "Breathe in," she said, "And breathe out." I did as she instructed, following her much more regular breathing, and then she said, "Blessed be."

When she stepped back I did feel calmer and quite determined not to let my fear be used against me.

I spoke the words of the incantation in a slow, clear voice. I felt the mirror handle warm up and grip my palm and then the light began to emanate, blue and spooky. Margaret stood behind me as the young woman emerged, fainter than before, and I said, "Meritamun. We want to help you. This is Margaret, can you see her?"

I angled the mirror but the girl said, "No. I only see you."

Margaret said, in a low voice, "And I see nothing but a bronze plate that needs a good polish."

Margaret said, "Ask her if her master has a name?"

Of course, why hadn't I thought of that? I repeated the question and the girl glanced behind her, as though he might be with her. "He is known as Athu-ba, the stealer of souls. He is a terrible demon, but he takes many forms. He tricked me by coming to me in the guise of my queen."

"Does he seek out witches only to destroy them?"

Margaret asked. Another excellent question, which I obediently repeated.

The witch in the mirror appeared to ponder the question, answering slowly, as though she'd never thought of it before. "No. I believe he takes their energy as his own."

He was feeding on witches, sucking out energy to use it against us. It was horrible and I began to feel sick. Before we could ask anything more, the picture wavered and Meritamun was gone.

Margaret took the mirror from me and looked at it more closely. "I'm sorry she was tricked like that. Our only hope is to destroy the mirror, which will kill her, of course." She sounded so matter-of-fact about another witch's death. But I'd become strangely fond of that poor young witch and I wasn't about to help destroy her. Not before we'd even tried to take out the evil demon.

"If we destroy the mirror and kill Meritamun, it won't stop him," I reasoned.

She looked at me, her head tipped to one side, as though considering. "No. It won't. It might save you, though. Are you saying you'll sacrifice yourself to save other witches?"

Not exactly. I wanted to save Meritamun, not end up destroying myself. But I could see it was a bind. "I want to vanquish this demon, that's what I want." I looked at Rafe. "Have you heard of this Athu-ba?"

Rafe was better than most search engines, and quicker. He nodded. "Athu-ba is a slightly obscure character in Egyptian mythology. He's got the head of a goat, the arms are snakes, and the body is human. He was called the soul-snatcher." Here Rafe looked thoughtful. "He was the son of Heka, god of magick, but he tried to kill his father and was banished from his household. He was known for stealing the souls of Egyptians before they could reach the afterlife."

Margaret looked thoughtful. "Who was that witch, exactly?"

"Meritamun. She said she was the Daughter of Amenemhat, the High Priest of Amun."

"He likes his women powerful, then."

I was shocked that she'd say that. Did she think I was powerful?

Margaret said, "Meritamun said he takes many forms. He came to her as her queen, someone she knew well." She gazed out of her kitchen window and her eyes narrowed. "Holding a different identity takes a great deal of energy. I'll make you a revealing potion. Anyone who ingests it, will be exposed as what they truly are."

That sounded like fun, stripping off the disguise so I'd be face to face with a soul-sucking demon. I was so glad we'd come to Margaret for advice! I looked at her. "And then what?"

"Then, you have to kill him. Obviously."

My day was getting better by the minute. "So, I reveal this demon in all it's terrifying glory, then kill it." I put my hands on my hips. "How?"

"Do you have much experience causing death?"

"No!"

"Pity." She turned to Rafe, "She's such a newbie. I don't know how we're going to stop him from killing her."

Rafe said, looking at her calmly, "You're the most powerful witch I know. If anyone can stop this warlock, or demon, or whatever it is, it's you."

She smiled, a tight, smug smile. "Well, that's true. Flattery still works. Of course, so much of magic is about illusion. Let me think."

She walked to a shelf of cookbooks and assorted volumes and selected an ancient, leather bound book that was similar to my family grimoire. She recited a quick spell and opened the book. As she pored over it, I realized that this was her spell book. She flipped back and forth, read a few pages and nodded.

Then she went to a drawer and pulled out a kitchen apron, blue and white striped heavy cotton, like a chef might wear. She pointed her finger at the cauldron and said, "Fire light, fire bright," and the logs beneath the cauldron, which I'd thought were for show, sprang to life. While the cauldron was heating, she went into her pantry and began selecting bits of dried herb and bark, jars of powder, some tiny, stoppered bottles of liquid. She assembled all this on the counter and then went back and returned with a very ordinary bottle of distilled water that looked as though it had come from a drug store.

She poured some of the water into the cauldron and then, checking her recipe now and then, began to add various ingredients. She didn't tell us what she was doing, and I was too nervous to ask. I smelled something woodsy, like wet mushrooms, as the concoction began to boil. She leaned over the bubbling pot, stirring it, then waved some of the steam toward her nose, closed her eyes and inhaled deeply. She leaned over the potion and recited a spell, but her words were low and quick, deliberately so, I believed, so we wouldn't be able to understand.

I looked at Rafe and he smiled at me. It was a smile that said, 'Don't worry. We've got this.' And it helped.

She breathed in the steam once more. "Yes," she said, "Yes, that's it." She glanced behind her to where I was standing. "Come, you stir it."

"Will that transfer its power to me?" I wondered aloud.

"No. I'm tired of standing here stirring a pot, that's all."

So, I took over the stirring and watched the dark potion bubble away.

"This is a revealing spell or potion. Athu-ba will most likely come to you in disguise. He could be one of your customers, a stranger you pass in the street; he could assume the guise of an old friend. If you can get him to drink a little of this liquid, you'll immediately see through the disguise."

I was getting serious heebie-jeebies at the idea that this soul stealer and destroyer of witches could pretend to be someone I knew. I thought of my mother, and the way she looked so strong, but she was the one who'd brought me the mirror. With an awful coldness around my heart, I asked, "Could he disguise himself as my mother?"

Margaret thought about it for a moment. "Theoretically, but not for long. You know your mother so well and there is a strong blood bond so it would take an enormous amount of energy for him to keep up that disguise. You'd have to be very distracted not to see through it. Look for a slight wavering around the edges."

I felt relieved. It couldn't be my mother, we'd spent all day together yesterday and she'd been entirely Mom-like. Her image hadn't wavered once. Neither had her conviction that I was wasting my time here in Oxford.

But someone I'd met or was about to meet would turn out to be the evil one. "And once I've revealed Athu-ba, then what?" Even saying the name gave me the creeps.

She didn't look as confident now, as she had when she chose the revealing spell, but she said, "Use the mirror. Reflect his evil back at him. And while you do that, recite this spell I'm going to give you."

"That's it? I make this terrifying monster look at himself in the mirror? Shall I comb his hair, too? Offer him a shave?"

"Lucy!" Rafe said, sharply. I couldn't help it. My sarcasm-fear response was deeply rooted.

CHAPTER 9

*T*he day was brightening now, and outside the birds were singing. I looked out the kitchen window and saw a black cat sitting on the window ledge outside. It stared in, green eyes blinking. I said, "Why your cat looks just like mine."

Margaret's blue eyes narrowed on me, the way Nyx's did, and then she turned and followed my gaze, out the window. "Well, well. You've a very devoted familiar there." She walked swiftly across the flag-stone floor, opened the multi-paned casement window, and in stepped Nyx.

I was surprised my cat had somehow travelled ten miles without even knowing where I was going, but, of course, Nyx had powers of her own. It was strange that she had followed me while I had that mirror, though. I thought she was scared of it.

Margaret picked her up and looked into her little face. "I believe I knew your mother."

Nyx made a noncommittal burp sound. Margaret

continued to hold the cat in her arms stroking it thoughtfully. "We were speaking of reflection," she said. "Yes, mirrors reflect ourselves back at us. We use the word 'reflection' when we speak of the past. We reflect on our lives, our deeds. A reflection is only an image. Not substantial."

I glanced at Rafe to see if he was following this patchy stream of consciousness but he merely raised his shoulders indicating he had no more idea than I did what Margaret was talking about.

"I can't promise it will work, but there is powerful magic in this mirror and the trick is to turn it on Athu-ba, make him reflect on who he is and what he's done."

I must have looked confused, for she said, "It's like Judo. Use your opponent's strength against them."

I had a feeling that my battle with Athu-ba would be a little more intense than a bout of Judo, but I nodded, letting her know I was following.

"The mirror is already enchanted, but we'll add an extra spell. When you reveal Athu-ba all you have to do is get him to look into this mirror while you cast a spell of your own. It's as simple as that."

Somehow I had a feeling that it wasn't going to be simple at all. I asked, "And if it doesn't work?"

"Then you die."

I couldn't fault her honesty. "What about Meritamun?"

"Who?"

"The woman trapped in the mirror. She's just a young witch and, through no fault of her own, she's been trapped for centuries, an instrument of his evil."

Margaret shook her head. "She was in the wrong place at

the wrong time and let her defenses down when she shouldn't have."

The potion was bubbling away and either I was losing my sensitivity, or the scent was diminishing. "I don't want to hurt her. Isn't there a way we can release her?"

She squinted at me and it was the oddest feeling, having both her and Nyx look at me with their eyes half closed, both tilted at the corners, green cats' eyes and blue. Margaret said, "Part of our code is 'Do what thou will, as long as it brings no harm.' Very well. We'll modify the spell a little." She wrote down the spell, checking her grimoire a couple of times, then nodded. "That should do it."

She handed me a perfectly ordinary piece of foolscap. Her handwriting was small and precise. I looked at the unfamiliar words. "What language is this?" Having grown up with the parents I did, I was conversant in ancient Egyptian, and could pick out words and phrases in Greek and Latin. This was none of those languages.

She said, "It's old English. Well, middle English, really." And then I could see the English roots of the words. "You're telling the spell to return to its maker in full force and to release the innocent vessel."

"Thank you. Do you think it will work?"

Her face gave nothing away. In the silence I could hear the liquid bubbling in the pot. "I honestly don't know. But it's the best I can do. If I were you, I would concentrate on eating well, try to get lots of sleep and practice your magic every day. The stronger you are, the stronger the spell will be."

It was so hard to practice magic when I had houseguests, but I didn't think she wanted to hear my feeble excuses, so I merely nodded. I'd find a place and time to practice, I'd have to.

To Rafe, she said, "Let me know how it turns out."

Which did not fill me with confidence. She didn't believe I'd be around long enough to tell her, myself, how it turned out. I packed the mirror back into its leather bag. She was still holding Nyx and, seeing how similar their faces were, I asked, "Do you shapeshift?"

She laughed. "That's a young witch's game. My back won't take it anymore."

I didn't have to ask if she had once shapeshifted into a cat; it was quite literally written all over her face.

She directed me to ladle the liquid from the cauldron into a stoppered glass bottle. She told me to fill two in case I dropped one. Once I had two glass bottles of a now clear and almost odorless liquid, I was more than ready to leave.

I thanked Margaret Twig and she wished me luck.

I reached out my arms. "Come on, Nyx, let's get you home."

Margaret's arms tightened around the animal. She shook her head and said, in a chiding tone, "Don't you know, there's always a price to be paid for a good spell?"

I took a step back, feeling foolish. "I'm sorry. I hadn't thought. I don't have very much money on me, but of course, just tell me how much it is."

She shook her head. "I don't want money, Lucy. I'm keeping your cat as payment."

I stared at Nyx, but, like Margaret, the cat's eyes gave nothing away. I couldn't stand to lose Nyx, not now when I was in danger and her magic was clearly more powerful than mine. "But-but, we've hardly had any time together, yet. I thought a witch's bond with her familiar was a deeply, personal relationship, like a marriage."

"Well, you can consider yourself separated, soon to be divorced." She smiled and I saw that her teeth were small and white and even. Like small rodents. I hoped she shapeshifted into a mouse and Nyx chased her into a hole.

I stood there, trying to think of a sensible argument, some way to get my cat back. I even contemplated giving Margaret Twig back her spell and the potion, but Rafe took my arm and began pulling me, physically, out of the room. He said, "Thank you, Margaret. We'll be in touch."

Then the vampire pretty much frog-marched me out of that cottage and back to his car. I was fuming. I barely noticed that dark clouds covered the sky and it was beginning to rain. "Stop dragging me. I'm going back for Nyx. She had no right!"

"It's raining. Get in the car," he ordered, then opened my door and stood there waiting for me. We had a short stand-off. The rain dampened his hair and splashed onto the shoulders of his jacket, but he didn't move. His gaze held mine and there was command as well as appeal in his eyes. I knew that if I tried to go back he'd stop me, which infuriated me even more.

With a sound of fury, I flung myself into the passenger seat of the car. When we were both inside the Tesla, with the doors shut, I turned to him, feeling angry and betrayed. "How could you let her steal Nyx?"

He had his cold, implacable look in place. "Lucy, that is a very powerful witch in there. She is also capricious. She decided to help you, but if you piss her off, she could mangle that spell and put you in worse danger."

Now he told me. "But Nyx is mine."

"Nyx won't be yours if you get killed," he said shortly. "Let's worry about getting you safely through this thing, and then we'll work on getting your cat back."

I felt marginally better that he seemed to think it was a possibility we could get Nyx back. Still, I knew that I was going to miss my familiar. Especially now, when I was under this death curse.

It was still early and, to my surprise, Rafe said, "Would you like to have breakfast?"

"Breakfast?"

His wintry eyes lightened. "It's a common ritual, where people eat something after they wake up, before they start their work for the day."

I responded to his charm, as I always did. I was still angry, but no longer with him. "Do you eat breakfast?"

He made a kind of back-and-forth motion with his head. "I ate earlier."

I'm certain he meant he'd made a withdrawal from the blood bank and not that he'd been out hunting during the night, but the attractive and repellent thing about Rafe was that I was never entirely sure. I was always aware that there was a bloodthirsty animal beneath the urbane surface of the antiquarian book expert.

He took me to a little café in Woodstock, the Cotswolds market town that was near Blenheim Palace. The café was busy with students on their way to school, a table of older women who looked as though they'd come from a brisk walk, and a young, dreamy guy who had a cup of coffee in front of him and his laptop open. Two dogs snoozed at the feet of the walkers.

The café was cozy and cheerful, exactly what I needed after the harrowing ordeal of the morning.

I was amazingly hungry and, remembering that Margaret had told me to eat well to keep up my strength, I ordered the full English breakfast. Two fried eggs, bacon, sausage, fried mushrooms, tomatoes, and toast. Oh, and a tiny ramekin of beans on the side. I asked for coffee as well.

I'd have sworn I could never get through such a plate of food, but still, I attacked it with gusto. I felt a little strange eating in front of Rafe when he only toyed with a cup of coffee, but I could see that he was enjoying watching me eat.

I believed that witches were particularly sensitive to the emotions of others and I felt, again, that sense of sadness or wistfulness as he watched me eat. I imagined him recalling all the flavors of food he no longer needed to sustain him.

After I'd satisfied the first pangs of my hunger, and could slow down a bit, I asked, "Do you think she's right? Do you think this Athu-ba will show up in the guise of a trusted old friend or some new acquaintance?"

One of the dogs had woken. It was a black spaniel and it wandered over to sniff Rafe. He leaned down to pat the dog, who hung out its tongue and gazed at him adoringly. "Well, I hardly think he's going to show up looking like a terrifying monster with horns. That would be a bit of a giveaway, wouldn't it?"

"All right, there's no need to be sarcastic. It's just that there are so many new people in my life. I don't where to begin, checking them all out."

"I'd start today. There's no sense waiting for him to make the first move."

This was something that bothered me. "Why hasn't he made a move yet? I've had the mirror for days."

He toyed with his coffee cup, turning it on the saucer. "Perhaps he enjoys the idea of frightening you first. Like a cat with a mouse."

I wished he hadn't said the word 'cat.' It made me think of Nyx, stuck in the arms of that cold Canadian witch.

"He might also be checking out the lay of the land. How strong a witch are you? Do you have powerful friends? Are you part of a coven?"

I frowned. "So, finding out I'm a fledgling witch with no powerful friends, and no coven, will be great news to the soul-sucker who's out to kill me."

He reached over and took my hand. "You do have friends. Don't ever forget that."

I felt a lump of emotion constrict my chest. "Thanks," I managed.

He seemed to hesitate and then said, "Also, I believe you are much more powerful than you know."

I nearly choked on my coffee. "Have you seen the mess I make of the simplest spells?"

He waved my words away with one hand. "Spells aren't everything. Anyone can memorize a book of spells. There's a power inside you. Why do you think Meritamun felt you? And Athu-ba wants to get rid of you? He doesn't do away with every discontented hippie who hangs a crystal around her neck and calls herself a witch. He targeted you for a reason."

"Mistaken identity?" I asked hopefully.

He shook his head. "You are from a very powerful line of witches. Margaret recognized it."

I made a rude sound, like a snort, indicating disbelief.

He raised one eyebrow. "Why do you think she took your cat?"

"Don't get me started on that. Who steals another person's cat?"

"Nyx is so much more than a pet. She's your familiar, and she's a powerful one. It occurred to me that Margaret is accustomed to being the most powerful and revered witch in Oxfordshire. Perhaps she confiscated your cat to limit your power."

"Well, then it was a rotten thing to do, especially when I'm under a death curse."

"You should accept the compliment. She clearly thinks you can beat this curse, even without your cat."

"Well, I'd rather do it with my cat, thank you very much."

"Don't lose your focus. Let's dispose of Athu-ba and then we'll worry about your familiar."

He'd used the term 'we' again and I quite liked it. Rafe was also very powerful. And I had no doubts that he was on my side.

I looked at him and I'm sure my eyes squinted the way Nyx's and Margaret's did when they were deeply considering something.

"What mischief are you plotting?" he asked, seeing my expression.

"You keep saying you're on my side, but you haven't said anything about how you're planning to help me."

"Because it's witch business."

I didn't believe him. "You're watching me at night, aren't you?"

He raised his eyes, looking startled. I knew I was right. If a vampire could look embarrassed, he did. Finally, he replied.

"Let's just say, as I'm walking through Oxford at night anyway, I put your flat on my route."

On some level, I think I'd known. Still, it was comforting to think of him out there, protecting me. "So, if I scream, you'll come to my rescue?"

He said one word. "Yes." And man, he packed a lot of assurance into that one word.

CHAPTER 10

*A*fter breakfast I felt better on every level. Apart from missing Nyx, I felt at least that I had some sort of plan, protection, and weaponry. Margaret Twig might demand very high payment for her services, but my instinct told me she'd given me the most powerful magic she could.

I glanced at my watch and saw that it was eight-thirty. I was pleasantly stuffed and the world seemed less frightening on a full stomach. I could even turn my attention to such mundane matters as my knitting shop.

"I'd better get back. I want to brush my teeth before I open the shop."

"Of course," he said, rising. I grabbed my purse to pay for breakfast and he stopped me. "My treat."

I could've argued, since he hadn't eaten or drunk a thing, but Rafe was old-fashioned, chivalrous, and very rich. I let him get the bill.

He dropped me off at the end of Harrington, which I appreciated as I didn't want my parents, or anyone else, seeing a man drop me off at my house in the morning.

I was about to go around to the flat's entrance, when I realized there were lights on in the shop. I couldn't believe Mom and Dad had forgotten to turn the lights out last night after their meeting. I walked in, ready to turn them out and jumped out of my skin when a cheerful voice said, "Good morning."

I put my hand to my chest. "Eileen. You frightened me."

"I said I'd be coming in early, if you remember. My bus gets here at twenty past eight." She was sitting in the visitor's chair, crocheting a small doll.

"Right, I remember." I watched her making magic with the crochet hook. "That's so pretty," I said, coming closer.

"They're poppets. I make them for my grandchildren. They love to play with the little dolls. Sometimes I make tiny animals, too. It's great for using up those leftover balls of wool."

The doll had a plump little body made of blue wool, with yellow wool for hair, tiny button eyes and a stitched on mouth and nose. Eileen was making the doll a tiny dress. I pictured a basket of these little dolls and patterns to make them in our front window. I'd need something adorable to draw visitors in, now that Nyx wasn't going to be in the window, anymore. I was suddenly overcome with sadness and anger at what that evil soul-stealer and Margaret Twig had taken from me, between them.

I needed to hide the deadly mirror, brush my teeth and, after a morning of stirring up potions, I needed a shower. "I'll just run upstairs for a few minutes. I'll be right back."

"You were out early, this morning." She ran her gaze up and down my body in a way that all but said, 'doing the walk of shame I see.'

I wanted to tell her that me showing up at eight-thirty in the morning wasn't what it looked like, but, first of all, she wasn't my mother, and, second, I'd sound more like a skank if I made excuses. I stuck to, "Yes, I had an early appointment." Which was true.

She put down her crochet and stood. Today she wore a blue skirt, crisp white blouse with a cameo brooch fastened at the throat, and over it she wore a blue cardigan patterned with knitted roses. She went to the cash desk and picked up a heavy-looking cloth bag and offered it to me. "If you're going upstairs, perhaps you can take the food?"

Right. We were having the Miss Watts for dinner tonight and Eileen had kindly agreed to cook. I walked over and peeked into the bag. Inside was a large, rectangular casserole dish, foil covered, another crystal bowl of trifle, salad in a bag, and two baguettes so fresh they were still warm.

"I can't believe you went to all this trouble. It's incredible, and far too much food for five people. Perhaps you'd like to join us for dinner?" I secretly suspected she'd deliberately made an extra-large meal so I'd invite her to join us. I wondered if Eileen was lonely now her husband had passed away and her grandchildren were getting older.

"Well, isn't that sweet of you to offer. But I always cook too much. I think it's nice to have the leftovers, and you never know when you'll feel the urge to invite someone else." She glanced at me sideways. "Perhaps, your young man?"

I refused to fall into that trap. I wasn't ready to discuss my love life or, in my case, my lack of one, with my new assistant. I said, "Well, if you change your mind, you know there's plenty of food and you'd be welcome to join us."

"Thank you, dear, but I promised my daughter I'd babysit her little ones tonight."

I took the food upstairs and put it on the fridge. My parents seemed to have got up, breakfasted, and gone while I was out. They had left me a note.

"Dear Lucy, we had an early breakfast meeting this morning. We've invited Pete and Logan and Priya for dinner tonight. Hope you don't mind a few extra guests at the table. Love Mom and Dad."

How had I not remembered that my parents were forever inviting stray archaeologists and grad students to share our food? I silently thanked Eileen for cooking twice as much food as I had imagined we'd need. Thanks to her, I didn't need to panic and run out and buy more.

I rarely used Gran's dining table, and had even thought of turning the dining room into a home office, but now I was glad to have it. The table would seat six comfortably and with the extra leaf, could accommodate eight, which was exactly the number we were having for dinner. Perfect.

Knowing my assistant was already downstairs, made me rush through a shower and change of clothes. At five minutes to nine, I walked back into my shop, this time wearing a hand-knit sweater that Hester had made me. Hester was an eternally annoying, sneering teenager, but she could knit. Whether out of simple boredom, or because she'd been encouraged by the other vampires, I had no idea, but she'd made me a gorgeous black and white pullover, with a slouch neck that looked good with a jean skirt, black tights, and short boots.

As I walked in, ready to open up the shop, I noticed that the vase with the daisies, lavender and rosehips was gone. In its place was a beautiful crystal vase containing three perfect roses. I went up and smelled them, and the scent was divine. "What beautiful roses."

"Thank you, Lucy. I pride myself on my green thumb."

I glanced around, "But what happened to the lavender and daisies?"

Eileen had half-wrinkled her nose before she realized what she was doing and straightened it. She said, with her placid smile, "Those things grow in ditches, dear. The rose is a proper flower, cultivated by civilized people. If the good Lord had meant us to bury our noses in wildflowers, he'd have made us all bees."

It was peculiar logic, but I wasn't going to argue with perfect blooms that looked as though they had come from an expensive florist.

Instead, I turned the 'closed' sign to 'open' and unlocked the front door. The bowl of wool in the front window still showed the impression where Nyx had slept. The cat had loved basking in the front window in various adorable, Instagram-worthy poses. A wave of sadness washed over me and I hoped Margaret would take good care of her.

I reached over and rearranged the balls of wool so I wouldn't be reminded of Nyx quite so much.

I raised my head, suddenly, hearing something. It was crazy, but I thought I could hear her meow. The sound was so clear I even walked outside and looked up and down the road, but there was no sign of my kitten. It was wishful hearing.

Fortunately, we were busy enough that day that I didn't have time to miss my cat. At least not too much. Eileen continued to be a model employee, up-selling my customers like a pro. One poor woman came in for a larger size of knitting needle and walked out with more than a hundred pounds' worth of wool, patterns, and various sizes of knitting needles.

It was only Eileen's second day and already I was contemplating giving her a raise.

Apart from my vampires, I'd never seen a more accomplished knitter. When I complimented her on her blue sweater, she said, "I had a lot of time to sit and knit in the hospital, when my husband was ill."

I nodded in understanding. It's a funny thing about knitting, people take it up for a variety of reasons, but when a loved one is ill it's a time-tested way to keep the hands busy and soothe the mind.

Eileen left at five, taking my deeply-felt thanks for her help in the shop and the food she'd cooked us, with her.

I ran upstairs and set the table. Then I went back downstairs and took the roses from the shop. They made a beautiful centerpiece on my grandmother's old oak table. I put in the leaf and found one of her old tablecloths. It was crocheted lace and it occurred to me that one of her undead friends had probably made this.

I put the shepherd's pie in the oven to warm, dumped the salad into a wooden salad bowl and added the homemade dressing Eileen had also supplied. The Miss Watts arrived exactly at six o'clock. I was happy they were here first, as I was able to explain to them that my mother and father had invited three archaeology grad students to join our feast.

Instead of being offended, I thought they both seemed relieved. They were clearly stiff with each other, and I imagined they felt that the more people present, the less obvious it would be that they were barely speaking. I felt so sad, but had no idea how I could help them. The first thing I was going to do when they left was search my grimoire for a reconciliation spell.

The next person to arrive was Pete, the Australian. He'd combed his hair and wore a clean blue shirt, the sleeves rolled up to show his tanned and very attractive forearms. He had two bottles of Australian wine with him, which he presented to me with a flourish. "I was awfully glad for the invite. Otherwise it was going to be another night in the pub for me."

I was surprised. "Don't you eat in the college dining room?"

"Oh, yeah, but not every night. Gets a bit dull."

If he was looking for excitement, he had not come to the right place. I explained to him, in a low voice, that we had two elderly spinsters joining us for dinner and he said, matching my low tone, "Don't you worry. I'm good with the old girls."

To my surprise he hadn't lied. He joined the two Miss Watts in the living room and introduced himself.

"And whereabouts in Australia are you from?" Mary Watt asked, clearly attempting to put him at his ease.

"I'm from Sydney, do you know it?"

Florence Watt said, "I had a dear friend who lived for a time in Australia." And then her face crumpled up and she began to cry.

Mary and I exchanged glances. Florence's dead fiancé had spent some years in Australia. I suddenly felt personally responsible that my parents had invited this man from Down Under to destroy the evening before it even began.

But, Pete rose to the occasion. He said, "I'm sorry. It's hard to lose a loved one. I lost both my grandparents last year." I thought he might cry too, and keep Florence company, but he managed a brave face.

Florence reached out and took his hand and I thought, strangely, that it did her good to realize she wasn't the only person grieving. They began to talk together in a low voice and Mary stood up and motioned me into the kitchen.

She sighed, sounding at her wits' end. "It's been so dreadful. Poor Florence. I don't know what she feels worse about, losing the man she loved, or that he duped her. She fell in love with the fantasy."

"I know. I think it's going to take some time."

Mary picked up a tea towel and folded it more neatly. "She still blames me, you know."

Having seen the two sisters together, and read their emotions, I was sure of one thing. "No. She doesn't blame you. There's a strain between you because she said some things she regrets, that she can never take back. She doesn't know how to tell you she's sorry. She thinks what she did was unforgivable."

It was Mary's turn to look as though she were about to cry. "Of course, I forgive her. I knew she didn't mean those terrible things she was saying."

"Then, I think it's up to you to open the subject. Tell her you didn't take any of it seriously and you're very sorry about what happened."

"I am sorry. I wish with all my heart he'd been the man she wanted him to be."

"I know."

She unfolded and refolded the same tea towel yet again.

"But, maybe she doesn't know. You're very wise for one so young, Lucy."

I was saved from answering by the bell announcing new arrivals. I ran downstairs and let in Logan and Priya. Logan had brought a case of beer and Priya presented me with another bottle of wine. I showed them both upstairs, wondering if my parents were going to remember they'd organized a dinner party. If they didn't, tonight wouldn't be the first time I'd ever entertained in their absence, on their behalf.

But, just as I was beginning to think they wouldn't show up, they came in, full of apologies. They'd attended a lecture by a dear friend they'd gone to university with and afterwards they've gone back to his office where they'd become deeply immersed in his latest paper on extending the reliability of radiocarbon dating. Naturally, they'd completely lost track of time.

Naturally, they'd invited Professor Hamish Ogilvie along with them to dinner. The professor was a lean Scotsman with red hair who blushed easily. He said, "Terribly sorry to barge in on you like this, but Susan insisted."

Once more, I blessed Eileen. I was able to truthfully say, "You're most welcome. We've got loads of food."

He said, rather sheepishly, "I didn't have time to stop for wine. This is from my private stock. From under his tweed jacket, he presented me with a bottle of scotch that was much older than I was.

As I took the whisky, I heard Margaret Twig's voice in my head. *"Athu-ba will most likely come to you in disguise. He could be one of your customers, a stranger you pass in the street; he could assume the guise of an old friend."*

I imagined he could also assume the guise of my parents' old friend. I'd like to radiocarbon date him.

Instead, I took the whisky into the kitchen and, while Mom and Dad were introducing their friend, I slipped into my bedroom, got one of the bottles of revealing potion, and slipped it into my pocket.

CHAPTER 11

*L*ogan and Priya were tucking into the beer, and Pete had opened one of the bottles of Australian red wine. It was a merry group when my mother and father and Hamish joined in. Hamish insisted on opening the scotch, which I knew was one of my father's weaknesses, and even my mother agreed to a small glass.

I was glad to see everyone having a good time. I went into the kitchen to put the last touches on dinner—and slip a little revealing potion into the food.

All of these people were new in my life. And here they were in my home having dinner. Any one of them could be Athu-ba. I took the stopper out of the bottle and sniffed. It smelled like water. I tasted it and, apart from the slightest hint of cinnamon, it had no flavor I could detect. After checking to make sure no one was coming, I sprinkled it over the shepherd's pie.

I felt terrible doing it, but Margaret had assured me the potion was harmless to anyone but a demon in disguise and, even then, all the liquid would do would be to reveal him in his true nature.

I figured anyone who came into my home in order to kill me was not someone I should worry about.

Pete suddenly appeared in the kitchen and asked, "What can I do to help?"

"Thanks," I said. "Can you shoehorn a ninth chair around the dinner table?" I gave him another set of cutlery and he took it and went out again.

I was prettying up the salad when he returned. I indicated the two baguettes. "You could cut the bread. Put it in that basket."

I was pleased to see that he washed his hands first and then took the bread knife and began slicing bread. I said, "Somebody brought you up right."

"With five kids in my family, and a mum who worked, we all learned to be useful in the kitchen." He glanced toward where the party was in full swing and then back at me. "I'm guessing you've learned to be handy in the kitchen, too."

I smiled. "It's not that they mean to be hopeless, but my parents have such gigantic brains, there is no room for practical matters in their heads. It was just lucky that I didn't turn out to be an intellectual too, or we'd never have eaten."

He laughed. "You're not like other girls."

Luckily, I'd already splashed the liquid over the shepherd's pie and when I looked at the surface there were no traces of potion to be seen. Pete had no idea how unlike other girls I was. "I'm not sure how to take that."

There was a kind of flirty banter between us that I couldn't deny. I was also very aware that such a gorgeous guy would have no lack of female companionship. He laughed. "I meant it as a compliment. I find you very interesting."

"Thanks," I said. "You're pretty interesting, too. For an archaeologist."

He winced. "I know. I should become a professional football player. That's how you get the chicks."

It was my turn to laugh. "I'm guessing that's not a problem you have."

"Maybe, I don't always get the ones I want."

I had no idea what to say to that, my flirting skills were sadly rusty, if I'd ever had any. Luckily, Priya chose that moment to come in and ask the way to the bathroom. I directed her and then suggested to Pete that we start putting food on the table. The party in the living room picked up their various glasses and adjourned to the dining table.

The shepherd's pie stretched nicely. No one turned out to be a vegetarian, or allergic to potato, or any of the things I had worried about. Eileen was as good a cook as she had led me to believe, as I discovered from my first bite. The shepherd's pie was delicious, the wine flowed and, in spite of the odd mix of people, amazingly, the conversation never flagged.

I tried to keep up but, really, I was much more interested in whether any of my dinner guests would turn into monsters before my eyes. I'd slipped the leather bag, containing the mirror, under my chair and I was on edge, ready, should the archaeology professor, one of the grad students, or even one of the Miss Watts, suddenly turn out to be the murderous Athu-ba.

I was certain the potion was tasteless, but, after a few bites of his shepherd's pie, Pete seemed to stop and really taste the bite that was in his mouth. Then, he looked up at me with a very searching look. I smiled innocently and dropped my gaze to my plate. Please, let it not be him, went through my mind. But still, if he was a demon in Australian sheep's clothing, I was ready.

But, Pete didn't turn into anything other than a charming, slightly sunburned Australian, Priya was more quiet than the others, but I thought she was just more reserved. Logan grew more loquacious, the more he drank, and Hamish's freckles became more pronounced as the bottle of scotch sank.

The Miss Watts were still the Miss Watts.

My parents were still my parents.

I was relieved, of course, but also mildly disappointed. I'd psyched up for this confrontation, and the longer I had to wait, the more my nerves would be stretched to breaking point.

After dinner was done, we moved on to dessert. The trifle was delicious, and Hamish told an amusing story about his nanny in Scotland who had condemned all things English except trifle, which, she said, was the only thing the English got right.

Mary and Florence Watt exchanged a glance and Mary said, "You tell it, Florence." And Florence had said, "No, Mary, you tell it so much better than I." And I realized I wouldn't need a reconciliation spell. All those dear ladies had needed was a night out in pleasant company to realize how very fond they were of each other.

In the end Florence and Mary told the story together, about how they'd both learned to make custard, and all the disasters of lumps, and burned pots, interspersing lines like, "And don't forget when poor Mother made you promise to keep stirring the pot while she went to get the mail, and you forgot, and when she came home there was burned custard all over the stove."

We all laughed heartily. And then I served coffee and tea, once again aided by Pete. While we were in the kitchen together, I asked, "Was everything all right with your shepherd's pie? You got a strange look on your face."

He looked at me again, in that same searching way. "No. There was a funny flavor I couldn't recognize. Probably a spice we don't get at home."

I nodded. "No doubt that was it."

PRIYA AND LOGAN left shortly after dinner, and Logan asked, "Coming, Pete?"

Pete said, "You go on. I'll help Lucy with the dishes."

Logan gave us both a knowing glance and nodded. "See you tomorrow, then."

The Miss Watts left next, and I could see they were both much happier than they had been when they'd arrived. Florence said, "Thank you for a lovely evening, Lucy."

When Florence went to say goodbye to my parents, Mary took both my hands in hers. "Thank you. I'm going to take your advice and have that chat with Flo." She looked toward her sister. "It's time."

Mom and Dad were in deep conversation with Hamish, while Pete and I did the washing up. He was easy company, and I was happy to have the help. When we'd finished putting everything away, he turned to me. "Walk me home?"

I raised my eyebrows at him. "Isn't it usually the boy who walks the girl home?"

He raised his brows right back at me. "Bit sexist, isn't it? Anyway, we're at your home. I'd love to walk you to your bedroom, but your mum and dad are right there. I don't want to lose a trip to Egypt."

I stifled a giggle and said, "All right. I'll walk you home. Just so I can get some air."

I told Mom and Dad I was taking a walk, but they were so intent on their conversation, I don't think they heard me. I put on a coat, made sure I had my key to get back in, and then Pete and I headed out into the night.

It was cold and quiet in the lane. The leaves and streets were wet from the earlier rainfall, but now it was dry. I looked up and there were no stars visible, and the moon was partly obscured by clouds. It looked spooky, as though black cobwebs had drifted across its face, like a Halloween moon.

Pete asked, "If I go on the dig with your folks, any chance you'll be there?"

I shook my head. "I'm no archaeologist. I run this knitting shop. That's my job."

"Oh, well, even if your folks do select me as part of the team, we won't be going for weeks yet. Can I see you again?"

Gorgeous guys did not usually ask me out. My not-so-spectacular boyfriend of two years had cheated on me, so I wasn't overconfident in the dating department. I wanted absolutely no misunderstandings. "Are you asking me on a date?"

He laughed, his white teeth gleaming in the night. "It's an old-fashioned way to put it, but yeah. I'm asking you on a date. How about dinner, tomorrow?"

Okay, so it seemed gorgeous guys did, occasionally, ask me out. Pete was easy to be with and handy in the kitchen.

And who knew how long I had before I faced the death demon? A night out sounded like a good idea. "I'd like that."

We were heading up Ship Street, and turned left on Turl toward Broad Street. I hadn't asked Pete which college he attended, but we were headed toward Balliol and Trinity. The night was still and cold and hardly anyone was out. It felt good to let my guard down. Pete hadn't turned into a crazed monster after he'd eaten the magic potion, so I knew I could trust him. We turned right on Broad Street and walked past the Sheldonian, with its ring of stone heads looking sinister in the near dark.

"They call those the Emperors," he said, then laughed. "I got that from eavesdropping on a tour guide." We walked past the Bodleian library, and turned right at Catte street. His college turned out to be one of the smaller ones, Barnaby College, where Mom had studied. He asked, "Do you want to come in for a drink?"

His eyes were full of tease and promise, but I shook my head. "I should get back. But I look forward to our date tomorrow."

If he was disappointed, he didn't show it. Instead, he put a hand under my chin and said, "I'm looking forward to it, too. You're a very interesting girl, Lucy Swift." And then he kissed me.

"Very interesting." Then he looked up and down the quiet road. "Should I walk you back home?"

I laughed. "Oxford's a pretty quiet town. I think I'll be okay."

"Good night, then. Until tomorrow."

"Good night."

He waved as he walked through the gates, and I waved

back, before turning around, in the direction we'd come. I hadn't gone far at all before I had another man walking by my side. This one wasn't warm and sexy; he was cold and furious.

"What are you doing walking out late at night, all alone? Did you not hear anything I said to you?"

"When have I been alone?" I challenged him, stopping and turning to face him. "I could feel you following us every step of the way, from the second we left my place. In fact, I might have liked a little privacy."

"So you could kiss a complete stranger?"

I was so irritated I pushed my face right into his. "Do you have a problem with that?"

His eyes were fire and ice at war. I watched his passion battle with the reality of our situation. I was mortal and he was vampire. How could that ever end well? Finally, he said, "For a woman whose life is in danger, you have a bad attitude."

We continued walking. "For your information, I sprinkled the revealing potion in their dinner. Guess what? None of them are Athu-ba."

"Or the potion didn't work."

I hadn't even thought of that. "What are you saying?"

He put an arm around me and pulled me out of the path of a drunk cyclist. "Did you put it in something hot?"

"Margaret didn't say I couldn't." I was so frustrated by these supposed rules that I only learned about after I'd broken them. "I sprinkled the potion over a dish that had just come out of the oven. I didn't put it back in again."

He shrugged. "Maybe the potions's heat sensitive. Or, it could have been neutralized by the potato."

I glared at him. I mean, I gave him the full treatment. I stopped walking, then took a step back. Put my hands on my hips. Oh, I meant business, when I glared, and he knew it. "I never said what we had for dinner. How do you know about the potato?" It was true, I'd sprinkled the potion on top of the cooked potato, on top of the shepherd's pie. But I was positive I had never told Rafe what we were having for dinner tonight.

He looked embarrassed and uncomfortable all of a sudden. "I might have glanced in the window."

I added outrage to my glare. "You'd better not make a habit of peeking in my windows."

He looked appalled at my not very subtle insinuation. "I'm not a Peeping Tom, if that's what you're insinuating. I knew you were entertaining, and I wanted to make sure you were safe."

I knew I'd be foolish to alienate the one person I could trust to keep an eye on me. Also, I didn't really think he peeked into my bedroom windows at night. Just in case he did, I determined to make sure the blinds were fully closed and that I wore my most demure pajamas to bed.

"I'm sorry," I said. "It's been a really long and stressful day."

He didn't look terribly sympathetic. "You'd better get used to it. Until this demon has been dispatched,, every day should be stressful for you."

Luckily, at that point we had reached my home. I said, "Thank you for walking me home. I can take it from here."

His hand touched my face fleetingly. "Good night, Lucy. Stay safe."

CHAPTER 12

$\mathcal{M}$y parents and I were sitting over breakfast when the call came.

They looked heavy-eyed and, frankly, hung over. I'd gone to bed, leaving them and Hamish in the living room with the bottle of scotch. The rise and fall of their voices had lulled me to sleep. I wasn't sure what time Hamish had finally left, I'd been asleep long before.

They gratefully drank the extra pot of coffee that I'd made and we were all on our various electronic devices, checking news, social media, or whatever our bent was, when my dad's cell phone rang. He flinched at the noise and then answered. He listened for a moment, puzzlement turning to horror, and then said, "I'll be right there."

His face was drained of color and his eyes wide as he looked at Mom and then me. "Logan Douglas suffered a heart attack last night."

"What?" My mother and I both said at the same time. "Is he all right?"

Dad shook his head. "It was fatal."

I couldn't believe it. I'd seen him only a few hours ago, laughing and heading home, his arm around Priya. "You mean he's dead?"

"I'm afraid so, Lucy."

My mother put a hand to her head. "But he was perfectly fine last night. Healthy and clearly enjoying himself."

Dad shrugged, looking helpless. "Sometimes it hits a young person like that. A hitherto unknown weakness in the heart or the circulatory system, always a tragedy."

Of course, my mind was racing. I thought about that potion I had fed to all my guests, a potion Margaret Twig had concocted. She was a powerful witch I knew nothing about. Had she given me, not revealing potion, but something that could be toxic? I felt hot and cold. Apart from my sorrow over poor Logan's death, I wondered if an autopsy would reveal whatever was in that mysterious potion.

My mother voiced the thought clanging in my head. "Could it have been something he ate?" She looked at me, her eyes wide. "He must have eaten his last meal, here."

My mind kept bouncing around. Even if Margaret's potion was sound, I hadn't cooked that shepherd's pie. I'd allowed an employee I barely knew to cook for my family and colleagues.

I felt sick. Absolutely sick. Had I inadvertently killed someone? The only thing I could think of was to get hold of Margaret and find out exactly what she'd put in that potion. I cursed myself for a fool. Why had I taken her on faith, without checking her out at all?

I had to be in the shop in less than an hour, but still I texted Rafe and told him I needed to go back and see Margaret again. Naturally, I didn't even know how to get hold of her. She probably had email addresses and phone numbers, but of course, I hadn't got any of them.

To my great relief he got back to me almost right away. He was tied up at the Bodleian until ten, and then he said he'd pick me up.

When I got down to the shop, Eileen was already there. Just seeing her placid presence calmed me down enormously. The shop was as neat as I'd never seen it and she was sitting in the visitor's chair, crocheting another poppet. She looked up when I came through the door from my flat. "Good morning, Lucy. How was your dinner last night?"

I must've shuddered visibly for she looked closer. "My goodness, what's happened? You look as though you'd seen a ghost."

Oh, my, how close she was to the truth. I'd seen Logan last night. This morning, he likely was a ghost. I said, "The dinner was wonderful. And your food was delicious, I can't thank you enough. But, unfortunately, one of the students who came for dinner died in the night."

She looked most concerned, as well she might seeing she had cooked the dinner. "Do you know how he died?"

"No. I imagine there will be autopsy and an inquest, but Dad thinks perhaps it was an aneurysm or something. One of those fluke events that kill young, healthy people."

Her face was creased with concern. "I'm sure it wasn't my food. Of course, if there was anything wrong with it, you'd all have fallen ill. And no one dies of food poisoning that quickly. At least I don't think they do."

Not being an expert in death or food poisoning I couldn't comment.

I walked up to the front door but couldn't face putting up

the 'open' sign. "I'm such a mess. I wonder if you'd mind watching the shop for an hour or so this morning? I need to get away and clear my head."

"Of course," she said in her motherly way. "I brought a little kettle from home and I've set it up in the back room. Why don't I make you a nice cup of tea?"

It was so nice of her, when she must know I had tea-making facilities upstairs. But I appreciated the gesture. "No. I've had too much coffee this morning already. But, thank you."

There wasn't time for more, as it was now time to open the shop which Eileen did, since I couldn't face it. She was so efficient, I was fairly confident the shop could run without me.

I got through the first hour of the day somehow. It was all a blur. I doubt I even served a single customer. I think I sat behind the counter, pretending to do inventory or some important task, while just staring at the blank screen of my computer. We weren't very busy, and Eileen efficiently took care of the few customers we did have.

At ten o'clock, I made my excuses and left her. Rafe picked me up in the lane behind the flat. As Eileen had done, he took one look at my face and asked, "Lucy, what's happened?"

I was surprised he hadn't heard. Rafe always seemed to know everything. But he was clearly both surprised and shocked at the news of Logan's death. "And you suspect Margaret?"

"I don't know. All I know is, I sprinkled her potion on the food and, within hours, one of the people who ate it was dead."

He nodded. Then he started the car and we drove out of the lane. "I'm sure I don't need to remind you that eight other people consumed the potion and were perfectly fine."

"But what if he had some kind of weakness, like an allergic reaction to whatever she put in that stuff? And what if it shows up in a tox screen? I'd be a murderer."

"I can't imagine Margaret putting anything dangerous or toxic into that potion, but I think you're right that it would be best to tell her what's happened and perhaps seek her advice."

What was this thing he had for Margaret? "Seek her advice? First, she steals my cat, then she kills my dinner guest. The only advice I want from Margaret is what I need to do to keep her out of my life."

He glanced sideways at me. "And yet, we're heading to see her right now."

"Only because I want some answers. And I miss Nyx."

It took a little longer to drive to Margaret's small village now that there was substantially more traffic on the road, but we still managed to pull into her gravel drive while the morning sun was glinting so prettily on the fading hydrangeas.

By the time we walked up the path, Margaret was standing at the open door. This time she wore red silk patterned with big black flowers. "I just heard. That poor boy."

"Margaret," I said, noting a strong scent of mint as I walked into the cool flagstone hallway. "What was in that potion?"

She looked a little taken aback at my question. "Just a little of this and a little of that. I don't give away my recipes."

I held onto my temper with effort. "Was there anything in that potion that could have killed Logan?"

She still looked puzzled and I said, "He had dinner at my place, last night. I sprinkled some of the potion on top of the shepherd's pie and fed it to him. And by this morning, he was dead."

"Good heavens. Then you were one of the last people to see him alive?"

"Yes. And he seemed fine. Perfectly healthy. He was an archaeology student. He wanted to go out on a dig with my parents. He was twenty-six years old. And now he's gone."

She led us into her kitchen and I saw that her cauldron was bubbling away with a mixture that smelled strongly of mint and, now that I got closer, of other fragrant herbs. I identified chamomile, lavender, and ginger and the rest was a blur on my senses.

She said, "Logan was a wizard."

I felt as though an electric shock had zapped all the way up my arm. "No, he wasn't. He was an archaeology student."

"And a wizard," she said, patiently. "Really, Lucy, you'd know all this if you came to the potluck, or at least joined our closed Facebook group. That's how I heard about Logan's death, this morning."

Rafe had said nothing, watching our interchange. Now, he spoke up. "What else did you hear?"

She shook her head. "That young man did not die of natural causes."

"What?" I pictured myself sitting in jail explaining how I'd sprinkled a mysterious liquid, given to me by a well-known local witch over Logan's food and, no, I hadn't bothered to find a what was in the potion.

CROCHET AND CAULDRONS

While my mind kept running back to the part where I found myself held responsible for the death, Rafe's mind was clearly going in another direction. He asked, "What do you think happened to him?"

She glanced at me sharply. Then she turned away and began stirring the contents of the bubbling cauldron with a very long-handled wooden spoon. "His coven in Glastonbury lost one of their oldest and most powerful members. I suspect it was Athu-ba who killed him. Logan, though young, was quite a powerful psychic. I think he had a vision that this demon was in Oxford and, perhaps, came to try and stop him."

My heart felt like an ice cube. I wanted to sit down, but there was no chair so I leaned against the cold, granite counter for support. "You mean that scary dude who's after me, killed Logan?"

She looked up from stirring. The steam had brought a flush to her cheeks. "As a theory, it makes more sense to me than an aneurysm."

She stirred the bubbling pot for another moment. In spite of myself, I was drawn to find out what she was doing. I breathed in. "That smells wonderful."

She smiled, and her cheeks bunched up like apples. "It's a tonic for pregnant women. It eases morning sickness, and the aches and pains that come with the condition. Of course, I put a little extra magic in it to calm the anxiety that pregnant women always face."

I kept looking around, trying to see my cat. Finally, I asked, "Where's Nyx?"

She took the spoon out and turned her back to the potion before answering. "She's in disgrace. She scratched my face

141

and neck when I tried to pick her up this morning." She eased away the red and black silk scarf that she wore, wound around her neck, and I could see faint scratch marks. I thought that Margaret must be quite allergic to the scratches for they were lined with something that looked like bubbles. I said, "Nyx never scratched me."

Margaret replaced the scarf and said, quite coldly, "She's no longer your cat. And she'd better learn that I'm her mistress, now."

As we left Margaret's cottage, I looked back and, in an upper window, I saw Nyx. Our gazes connected and the cat put out her paw and began banging on the window, asking to be freed. I drew Rafe's attention to my imprisoned familiar. "That horrible, old witch has Nyx trapped. We have to get her out of there."

Rafe took my eagerly pointing hand, clasped his around mine. "Right now, you need Margaret, you need her strength, her magic, and her cooperation. Once this confrontation is over, then we can think about getting your cat back. Understood?"

It was pretty much what he'd said the day before. He didn't know how much I missed my cat, but I conceded that he might be right. Thanks to Margaret, I knew Logan had been a wizard.

Besides, I comforted myself by recalling the bubbling near the site of the cat's scratches. It looked very much as though Margaret was allergic to her stolen cat.

As we drove away, Rafe said, "The good news is that Margaret's magic potion didn't kill your friend."

I replied, "And the bad news is the same demon who's after me, killed Logan, without a fight."

CHAPTER 13

*H*e reminded me that he was never far away and he added, further, that he had recruited some of the other members of the vampire knitting club to keep an eye on me. "Any time, day or night, you're never alone. One scream and somebody will be there, instantly."

It was comforting, if somewhat unnerving, to know that a whole nest of vampires was that tuned in to me. But, I thanked him and went back to work. I wished I had known Logan was a wizard who was possibly after the creature now stalking me. It would have been so nice to exchange confidences with someone like me, and perhaps pool information. I wondered how Logan had known about the demon, and if Meritamun had somehow been involved in causing his death.

When I got back the shop, I realized that the vampire knitting club took surveillance duties seriously. I blinked, on finding Clara deep in conversation with Eileen about her latest project, a knitted sweater-coat. She appeared to be struggling to knit the collar.

When I walked in, she gazed at me, as though having

trouble placing me, and then said, "Lucy, isn't it? The new owner of the shop? I was telling Eileen, here, how much I used to enjoy coming to Cardinal Woolsey's when your grandmother ran it." She looked around as though she hadn't seen the place in years, when she was up here at least twice a week for meetings, and only lived downstairs.

Now, she sighed, with a mix of nostalgia and sweetness. "Cardinal Woolsey's never changes. It's up to you, now, Lucy, to continue the fine tradition."

I blinked and said, "Yes. I mean, my grandmother was a wonderful woman. I can never fill her shoes."

"No. But you'll do your best, I know." Then she smiled sweetly at my assistant. "Eileen's been helping me interpret this fiendishly difficult pattern. I was going mad, thinking I wouldn't finish my sweater before Christmas. I do want to wear it."

Clara rarely bothered with patterns, so it was a real active sacrifice for her to pretend to be confused, and to be guided by a mere mortal. She managed to drag out her visit for a little longer and then she left. It seemed only moments later that one of the male knitting vampires, Alfred, walked in. He did a good job of looking slightly bewildered, as though he'd never held a pair of knitting needles in his life, when I had personally seen him turn out a pair of exquisite knitted gloves in a complicated shell pattern in the space of one evening. He smiled at us both, vaguely, showing no recognition when his gaze rested on my face.

Eileen went forward. "Can I help you?"

I listened, quite entertained, as he described how his wife was feeling poorly and so had sent him to get extra wool as she had run out. He did an excellent job of dragging out his visit, since he couldn't remember what kind of wool she needed, what sort of a jumper she was working on, even what color. Eileen very obligingly pulled out nearly every leaflet we had in the shop and showed him a variety of different wools. In the end, he decided to choose an entirely new pattern and enough wool to knit the entire thing. Since I suspected it was a project he planned to do himself, I simply enjoyed the transaction.

And that's how it went for the rest of the day. No sooner had one vampire left than another would come in. They'd come in to browse, or they'd pass the time asking questions, dragging out the shopping experience, and Eileen's patience, for as long as possible.

Even though I felt I was in no danger in the middle of the day in a public shop, I loved their kindness. Especially as most of them had interrupted their sleep in order to take the shift.

My mother worried that I didn't have very many friends, but she was wrong. They might be slightly unusual, but these knitting vampires sure acted like friends.

About three o'clock I glanced up when the door opened, to see, not another of my undead knitting friends, but DI Ian Chisholm, looking slightly more serious than usual.

My heart sank as he came straight up to me and said, "Lucy," in his crisp, police officer tone.

"Ian," I said, then I stalled. I couldn't say 'How nice to see you,' or ask if I could help him, since he knew that I knew why he was here. So my words just petered out and I looked at him.

He obligingly picked up the conversation ball that I'd

dropped, wet and chewed, at his feet. "I need to ask you a few questions, in a professional capacity."

I nodded, feeling sick and hollow inside. Even though Margaret had assured me that it was the demon, and not her potion, that had killed Logan, I wasn't completely convinced. I asked Eileen if she would watch the shop for little while, and, of course, she said she would. Her eyes nearly popped out of her head as she realized I was about to be questioned by the police. I only hoped my connection to a crime wouldn't make her rethink her employment with me. I thought, on top of everything that was going on right now in my life, losing Eileen would be the biggest disaster of all.

I took Ian upstairs and asked him if he'd like anything to drink, but he declined. My parents were out and even Nyx was missing, so the place was curiously still and quiet.

He said, "I understand you had a dinner party here, last night."

I winced. "I wouldn't call it that, exactly. Mom invited the Miss Watts for dinner and then invited three of the grad students that are planning to help on the archaeological dig in Egypt. And then she and Dad invited a colleague."

"You heard what happened?"

I nodded. "My father received a call this morning that one of those three students was dead."

He didn't say anything, only looked at me. I knew it was a cop's trick to get me to keep talking and, with me, it always worked. "I feel just terrible. I imagine the meal he had here last night was the last one he ever ate."

He nodded. "Can you tell me what you served for dinner?"

Of course, I told him, and that we'd all eaten the same thing. I took a deep breath. "How did he die?"

He shook his head. "We don't know. There are no marks on the body. No obvious physical signs of illness or trauma. We have to treat this death as suspicious until we find out otherwise."

"I understand." I liked Ian. I wished I could tell him everything I knew, but he was a man of the physical world. He dealt in black and white, crime and victim, guilt and innocence. How could I tell him that there were creatures from antiquity out causing havoc? That I was a witch and Logan had been a wizard?

I couldn't. It was hopeless.

He asked, "How did he seem to you, last night?"

I thought back to the evening. "He was jolly. Everyone was. He brought beer and some of the others brought wine and scotch and it just turned into one of those surprisingly fun evenings, considering what an odd collection of people we were." I walked Ian to the dining table, still with its nine chairs crammed together. "He sat right there," I said, pointing to where, just last night, Logan had been telling stories and laughing along with the rest of us.

"Would you let me know what you find out about Logan? I feel awful that he died the same night he had dinner at my place."

"If it's any consolation, everyone I spoke to remarked on what an entertaining evening they had here. At least you made his last evening a good one."

I didn't feel very consoled, but it was kind of him to say that.

"Tell me everyone who was here, and where they sat."

I did. Seeing it all again, through his eyes.

He hesitated, then asked, "Did there seem to be any animosity between Logan and anyone else last night?"

"Quite the contrary. He and Priya left together. I don't know if there was a romance going on there, or whether they were just friends, but they seemed close."

"Had he known any of those people before?"

"I don't know. I think he recognized Pete, the Australian, from somewhere. But I really don't know."

He nodded and asked, "This is purely routine, what were your movements last night? After dinner?"

"Well," I said, "Logan and Priya left after dinner. Around nine o'clock, I think. Then the Miss Watts left after that. Maybe half past nine, or ten."

"And the other student? Pete, I think you said his name was."

It was ridiculous, but I felt heat climbing into my cheeks. I didn't want to blush in front of Ian. He and I had never even had a date, so to feel embarrassed telling him that I spent some time alone with another man was ridiculous. But I could tell myself that all I liked, and I still felt the heat of a blush rising to my cheeks.

"Pete stayed later. He helped me do the dishes. My parents and their friend, Hamish Ogilvie, were in the other room still talking."

"And what time did Pete leave?"

"Closer to eleven."

"And, then, what did you do?"

"I walked back with him to his college, Barnaby College."

He looked at me. "The same college where Logan was staying?"

"I think so. But of course, I didn't see Logan. He'd left earlier."

"And did you go in with Pete?" His voice was level, with only the slightest interrogatory inflection, but I felt his keen interest in my answer. I was pleased I could tell him that no, I hadn't gone in. "I walked back home again."

"Let me get this straight. You left your home and walked Pete back to his college and then turned around and walked back again?"

It did sound very peculiar when he said it like that. I put my arms up helplessly. "We'd all been drinking, it seemed like a good idea at the time. I thought some air would be good for me. It was a very pleasant evening for a walk. So, yes, I walked down to the college and back again."

"And that's all you did?"

Well if he wanted every detail of my evening, I guessed he could have it. I said, "Pete kissed me."

I wasn't sure if he was annoyed or amused at my answer. It was hard to tell when he was in serious detective mode. He said, "I see. And this happened outside the college?"

"Yes. As I told you, I did not go inside."

"And then you walked back home."

"Yes."

"Did you see anyone?"

I hesitated. A moment too long. I wanted to tell him that, yes, I had walked home all alone but it wasn't true. I said, "Rafe happened to be out on the street last night. I bumped into him and we walked back here together."

"I see. You were well-escorted, then."

"I was."

He looked at me, then. He had a way of looking at me that made me want to tell him all my secrets. That was what made him so good at his job. His moss-green eyes were intent. "Is there anything at all you can tell me that might help in our investigation?"

Apart from the fact that Logan had apparently been a wizard and was chasing a very bad supernatural character, I didn't have any information. And, somehow, I didn't think that getting Ian Chisholm involved in witches and wizards was going to be particularly helpful to any of us. So I stuck with, "No. I'm sorry."

He shook his head, looking puzzled. "I don't know what it is about you, Lucy, but you seem to draw disaster to you."

Oh, he had no idea.

I had a sudden thought. "Have you spoken to Pete, today?"

"Yes. Why do you ask?"

"I wanted to make sure he was okay. That's all."

"He looked well, when I spoke to him," he said, "but you can ask him yourself how he's doing. He told me you two were having dinner, tonight."

I put my hand to my mouth. "Oh, my gosh, we are. It's been such a crazy day, I almost forgot."

If a smile can be sarcastic, he gave me a sarcastic one. "I don't think he's forgotten."

Then he left. And I wondered what that was supposed to mean.

～

I KNEW that if the evil Egyptian demon had killed Logan, he was closing in on me, so I kept the mirror and the potion that Margaret had made for me close by for the rest of the day, but thankfully no one appeared to try and kill me.

I called that a win, that and the fact that sales were way up. Every single vampire who'd come in to waste time in Cardinal Woolsey's ended up being pressured by Eileen, the super salesperson, into buying something. Usually, more than they intended to buy. I was glad they were all so rich or I might have felt guilty.

I missed my grandmother. Of all times for her to be away, this was the worst. I needed her calm, good sense, and her guidance. She'd been a witch, she'd know what I was going through, maybe help me with spells to keep me safe. My parents were great and I loved them, but I couldn't tell them the truth about what was going on. And besides, no one gave good advice like my grandmother.

She'd have made me feel better. I'd always thought I'd have enjoyed more attention from my parents if I'd been about two thousand years old, wrapped in linen cloth and they'd dug me up instead of giving birth to me. It wasn't that I blamed them; they were wonderful people, just slightly obsessive about the archaeology.

Apart from Gran, I missed Nyx. Even though I knew all my vampire friends were keeping a close eye on me, I was enough of a witch that I missed having my familiar around. She might only be a young and fledgling familiar, but I was a young and fledgling witch, so we matched. I hated to think of her trapped upstairs in Margaret Twig's stone cottage. I bet Margaret didn't feed her the special tuna she liked.

As soon as I'd dealt with this demon, I had a spot of cat-napping in my future.

~

AFTER IAN LEFT, I walked into Cardinal Woolsey's to find Eileen explaining to Silence Buggins that Lucy would be back soon. It was a very odd picture these two made. Eileen looking every inch the comfortable pink-clad matron and Silence looking like she'd stepped out of a Victorian photograph. I could only suppose that people in Oxford either thought she was an actress or perhaps a member of some religious sect that insisted women be covered from neck to ground in natural fabrics.

Silence was, as usual, chattering up a storm. Eileen had a slight dazed look on her face and I thought even her endless patience was being stretched.

Eileen saw me first and said, with relief, "There she is. Here's our Lucy back."

Silence turned and looked clearly relieved. I don't know what my vampire body guards' signal was to call for help but I got the feeling that she had been close to pulling whatever alarm bell they'd agreed on.

She said, "Good afternoon. I'm so pleased to see you." She placed her small, white hand to her chest. "I've been having such trouble with this piece of knitting. But your assistant very kindly helped me sort it all out."

"I'm so pleased," I said. "And you're in good hands, she's a much better knitter than I am."

This wasn't saying much, of course, nearly everybody

who'd ever picked up needles or a ball of wool was a better knitter than I was.

A couple of young girls about twelve came in at that moment with their mothers. Silence looked at them with deep suspicion, as though they might suddenly morph into killers. When, instead, one of the moms explained that the girls wanted to learn to knit Silence said, "I think I'll just settle on this nice chair here, and work on my knitting. Then, if I run into trouble again, one of you nice ladies can help me."

I said that was fine and suggested to Eileen that she go and have a break while I dealt with the novice knitters. She glanced at Silence. "Perhaps I will pop out and get some air." When she left, she glanced back through the window, as though deeply hoping Silence wouldn't be there when she returned.

Silence seemed to take a real interest in the young girls. She said, "Oh, what lovely young ladies. You must be very proud. And what a fine pastime knitting is. So ladylike."

The mothers nodded and thanked her, then ushered their kids over to where I was sorting out some of the easier knitting patterns. Thanks to Eileen, I was able to suggest that they start with a simple square, but once they'd done that, it was an easy step to a scarf.

Silence had been listening, and now she said, "Yes, a scarf is very important, particularly when the weather grows chilly. Look how fine their skin is. And the throats still unmarked, not a wrinkle to be seen."

I didn't like the way this Victorian vampire was eyeing those sweet young throats and probably thinking about how delicious their sweet, young blood would taste. I always kept a good supply of solid wooden knitting needles and a couple of extra fat ones that I had sharpened back when I was particularly nervous about the vampires. I made sure they were within easy reach just in case.

I'm not sure whether he had some sixth sense, or whether he felt he'd inflicted Silence on us long enough, but just as Silence had risen from her chair to 'help' the girls choose a simple pattern, Rafe appeared. I sighed with relief and eased my grip on the sharpened wooden needles.

At the sight of Rafe, Silence picked up her knitting. "Well, I'd better be on my way." His appearance must have flustered her because, instead of going out the front door, she began heading toward the back room, which led to the trapdoor into the tunnels.

I ran after her and said, "Miss, the door's that way."

She looked startled and then laughed, a high, artificial sound. "Oh, how silly of me. I don't know whether I'm coming or going, some days."

When she left, I breathed a sigh of relief.

The girls and their mothers were happily poring over patterns, and arguing about colors for a scarf. At least one of the mothers seemed to be quite an experienced knitter, so I left them to it and said to Rafe, "I think Silence was getting peckish."

He glanced out the window, where she was walking quickly toward Rook Lane. I knew there was an entrance to the tunnels partway down the lane. Hopefully she'd visit their private blood bank before coming up here again.

"I shouldn't have let her take a shift, but she wanted to be helpful. You know what she's like."

"I do. And I appreciate the thought, but she was eyeing those two girls like they were a very tasty midnight snack."

"I'll have a word with her."

He asked me how I was holding up and I told him, quite honestly, that my nerves were stretched to breaking point. Actually, I think they'd snapped, like overfilled balloons.

He said in a low voice, "I want you to stay inside tonight. I'm trying to find out more about Logan's murder. The initial autopsy report is inconclusive. They can't find a mark on him. That is some very powerful magic."

"I can't stay in tonight. I have a date."

He rolled his eyes. "Do you really think this is a good time to begin a relationship?"

I rolled my eyes right back at him. "Do you really think you are in a position to give me dating advice?"

He glared at me for a long, steely moment. "Where are you going on this date?"

"I don't know."

"All right. I'll find somebody to keep an eye on you."

"Oh great, just what I need. A chaperone. This feels just like the fifties."

He looked at me puzzled. "The fifties?"

"Yes. The 1850s."

I was tempted to cancel dinner. The idea of being spied on by the undead was enough to put anyone off their food. Especially if he sent Silence Buggins. But, then I thought about Pete and how sad he must be right now. At least we could talk about the loss. I felt like I owed him that.

Rafe picked up a knitting magazine and, while pretending to flip through it, asked, "Where is your assistant?"

"I think Silence almost literally talked her ear off. I told Eileen to go and have a short coffee break. She should be back soon."

He nodded and began to look at shelves as though he were thinking about beginning a knitting project. I suppose it was rather sweet that he wanted to keep such a good eye on me, but it was also somewhat controlling. The door chime went off and I turned to greet my new customer and, to my surprise, saw the older gentleman who had applied to be my assistant, not so many days ago. Given his allergies to wool and cats, I was surprised to see him back in Cardinal Woolsey's. He looked a bit surprised, too. "Mr. Cruikshank. How are you?"

He looked as harried and woebegone as before. He was neatly dressed, like an accountant off to work, and still carrying that attaché case. He said, "I took the liberty of taking a decongestant before I walked in." He glanced around the shop, no doubt looking for my cat, but, sadly for me, she wasn't there.

I said, "Can I help you with something?"

"Yes. My wife said I didn't try hard enough in our interview. She thinks I should learn how to sell myself." When he said 'sell myself' he lifted his fists and made a motion as though he was banging on a heavy door. I could see him being forced to practice that gesture in front of his no-doubt horrible wife.

Rafe turned to look at him and narrowed his eyes. Before I could tell the man that I had already hired an assistant, Rafe asked, "Why don't you make Mr. Cruikshank a cup of tea, Lucy? I'll keep an eye on things out here. He can practice his interviewing skills on you."

I turned to stare at Rafe and saw him cut his eyes very quickly to the bag where I kept the mirror and the potions Margaret had given me. Was he seriously thinking this sorry-looking, henpecked man was Athu-ba, stealer of souls? But then, of course, if evil could choose a shape, what better one than someone as nonthreatening as poor Ned Cruikshank?

The older man perked up. "A cup of tea would be most welcome. It's very hard work looking for a job. Especially at my age."

I put on the kettle and made tea. Eileen had brought in, not only a kettle, but two china tea mugs for us, both patterned in roses, and some tea bags, sugar and some single portion containers of long-life milk.

Mr. Cruikshank took me through his resumé, line by line, elaborating on the extra responsibilities he'd held, beginning as a junior accountant and working his way up to management. I interspersed a few questions, allowing him to expand on his answers. He began to grow visibly more confident as I encouraged him.

I slipped a little of the revealing potion into his tea, putting the bag with the mirror on my lap and practicing the spell Margaret had given me. I was glad Rafe was in the other room, because the thought of confronting an evil demon who'd already killed a man, just last night, was terrifying.

But, Mr. Cruikshank didn't turn into any kind of monster as he drank the tea. If there was any change, it was that he grew into a more confident individual. After about fifteen minutes, I said, "I'd hire you in a minute, if I were an accounting firm looking for an experienced professional."

As he'd been speaking with me, Ned Cruikshank's voice had become increasingly nasal, as though he were coming down with a cold. Now, he sneezed, put his teacup aside, and said, "Thank you, Lucy. I feel so much better now. I know exactly what I'm going to do."

I smiled at him. "I suspect it won't have anything to do with working inside a shop that sells wool."

He chuckled. "No, it certainly won't. You've helped me enormously. I see, now, how accomplished I am. What I'm going to do, is volunteer for a charity that would appreciate my accounting skills. I don't need the money; I've got a nice pension. My wife simply wants me out of the house."

"I think that's an excellent idea," I said. "You'll be really helping people who need it, and using your skills and experience."

He seemed so pleased with himself at that burst of bravery that he was a like a new man as he left the shop.

I shook my head at Rafe even though he could clearly see that Mr. Cruikshank wasn't a monster.

Rafe left as soon as Eileen returned and the rest of the day was uneventful, if you didn't count the constant stream of vampires coming in to check up on me.

When closing time came I did a mental accounting and calculated I'd had more vampires in the shop that actual humans.

CHAPTER 14

I went back upstairs and found my mother alone, busily working on her computer. She looked up, blinked a few times before realizing she was wearing her reading glasses, and pushed them onto the top of her head.

"Lucy, your dad's got a dinner meeting that will probably go late. I thought we'd go out ourselves. It's too grim having dinner here, when that poor boy ate his last meal with us last night."

"I'd love to, Mom, but I already have plans for tonight." Then I thought of her all alone up here and felt bad. "But I could cancel, if you want me to."

When I told her that Pete had asked me out for dinner, her face lit up. "He's so charming, and an archaeologist, too."

I thought that his being an archaeologist trumped his niceness in my mom's eyes. I insisted that I could cancel if she didn't want to be alone but she assured me she had lots of work to catch up on. There was plenty of food in the fridge, so she'd be fine.

She went back to her computer while I went upstairs to shower and get ready for my evening.

I put on my best jeans and, after hesitating, I chose the exquisite midnight blue V-neck silk knit with the bell sleeves that Sylvia had knit me. She'd told me to wear it on a date, and this was a date. I fastened the diamond necklace, the perfect accessory as she'd no doubt known. I took a selfie, so I could show her when she returned from Dublin.

I styled my hair the way the salon stylist had showed me, applied a little makeup and then debated whether to take my potions and the mirror along with me. I already knew that Pete wasn't the evil demon, since he'd eaten the potion-sprinkled food last night and been fine. Also, the mirror and potion were bulky so I'd have to take a larger bag, which was a nuisance. However, I'd be out in public. I'd be vulnerable.

So, instead of the much cuter small bag, I now had to take a large one. I'd look like one of the university students carting her books around.

At least I'd fit in.

Pete had told me he'd pick me up for our date and, given that I was under strict instructions not to go out alone, I'd agreed. When the bell rang, I said good-bye to Mom, who was so deeply involved in her research, she barely registered me speaking to her. I looked at her with fond exasperation.

"Mom. Don't forget to eat something."

"I won't," she said, vaguely, and waved me off with one hand.

I ran downstairs and, when I opened the door, Pete gave a low whistle of approval. "You really are a beauty."

"You are a flatterer." Still, what woman doesn't want to be told she's beautiful, even if it's stretching the truth?

Pete looked as good as always, though I thought he'd had his hair trimmed and he'd definitely shaved. He wore a crisp, blue shirt with his jeans and a well-worn leather jacket. "Where do you want to go? I found a few places, online, but I reckon this is your town."

I thought quickly. If I was going to be under the watchful gaze of a vampire or two, I could make it easier for them by suggesting a venue where they wouldn't be quite so obviously out of their element. "Do you know the Eagle and Child pub?"

"The Bird and the Baby?" He gave the pub its colloquial, jokey name. "Sure."

"It's got a great atmosphere, and the food's good."

"Sold to the lady in the beautiful blue sweater."

As we walked, I kept a hand on my bag, ready to pull out the mirror, the way a gunslinger in the Old West might go for their gun, if threatened. Pete kept up a light, flirtatious conversation, but I sensed a tension in him. Or, perhaps he was reacting to the tension I could feel in my whole body.

We were about to cross Beaumont Street, toward the Ashmolean and were waiting for the light to change, when there was a scuffle of feet and a young guy pushed past me, jostling me. I had my hand in my bag, clasping the mirror almost instantly, when I felt myself shoved bodily. I cried and stumbled back and realized that Pete had pushed me behind him and was standing aggressively, blocking me from harm.

In the second it took me to react, I realized we were in no danger. It was just a young guy in a 'husband to be' T-shirt, with a plastic ball and chain around his ankle, already quite drunk. Several of his mates came running behind him, laughing.

Pete turned to me then, and grinned. "Bloody stag nights. You all right?" The *no worries, mate* Aussie was back.

"You almost threw me to the ground."

"Sorry, about that. I've spent too much time in dodgy places. I frighten easily."

I readjusted the strap of my bag over my shoulder. "It's nice to know I'm safe, in case one of those bachelor parties turns deadly."

He laughed and put an arm around my shoulders, and we made the rest of the walk to the pub without incident.

The Eagle and Child drew students, tourists, and regulars, so it was usually busy. J.R.R. Tolkien and C. S. Lewis famously used to sit in this pub and talk books. Maybe that's why I'd chosen this pub. The ghosts of Gandalf and Bilbo Baggins were comforting reminders that smaller, weaker creatures could win against big evil.

We toured the whole pub before coming across a couple who were just leaving. We sank gratefully into their still warm seats, pushing empty glasses and plates to the side. We were in a wood-paneled alcove and when I looked on the wall, Tolkien himself looked gravely down at me from a photograph.

"What do you fancy to drink?" Pete asked me. I chose a glass of white wine, promising myself to stick to a single glass, as I needed my wits about me.

He went up to the bar to order drinks, and while he was gone, a young woman with a tattoo of a serpent around her upper arm cleared the table and wiped it down.

I glanced around the pub, my hand resting on my bag. No one seemed suspicious, and no one seemed to be paying me any attention, apart from a lone man who'd just walked in. I watched Rafe check out the other patrons as I had just done, before heading over to stand in line at the bar.

Pete came back with our drinks. "I like this place. It's exactly what you think an old English pub will be." He raised his pint. "And the beer selection is good."

He chatted away, charming and flirtatious as always, but his gaze was restless, looking around as often as he looked at me. Now, maybe I hadn't been on as many dates as some girls, but I knew when a man was interested. There was a certain intensity in his gaze when it rested on you. I felt it when Rafe looked at me, I definitely felt it when Ian Chisholm looked at me—the way a soap opera hero looks at the woman he's in love with, the one who's either about to betray him or die. Pete looked as though he were acting attraction rather than feeling it.

We studied the menu and Pete said he thought the fish and chips looked good. I was having trouble even concentrating on the menu, so I agreed that sounded good and I'd have it too. He went back to order our food and I noticed two more members of the vampire knitting club come in. Alfred, looking spiffy in a forest green cable knit pullover he'd only begun last week, and Christopher Weaver in one of his endless exotic hand-knitted waistcoats, worn under a black suit jacket with jeans.

Pete returned and, while we waited for our food, I told him how sorry I was about Logan.

His veneer of easy-going charm slipped for a second and I saw real anger in his gaze. Then the mask was back. He said, "Terrible thing. I heard it was a suspected heart attack. Did you get anything more?"

I shook my head. "The police interviewed me, so they're

considering all possibilities." He nodded, sipped his beer and his gaze scanned the room. I said, "I got the impression that you two knew each other, before."

"Not really. We ran into each other, at a music festival."

He brought the conversation back to my parents and the dig. It was all very delightful and superficial, but I was becoming increasingly irritable, not knowing who was friend and who was foe. Our food came and while we were crunching through the delicious battered fish and he was telling me a somewhat amusing account of his first dig, I suddenly lost all patience. I leaned over and put my hand over his.

He was so startled he stopped talking and stared at me. Good. I had his complete attention. "What's going on, Pete? Who are you, really?"

He looked at me, searchingly. "What do you mean?"

"You've spent more time looking around the pub tonight, than looking at me, hardly flattering on our first date. You've barely touched on the mysterious death of your colleague last night, and on the way in, when that drunk stumbled in front of me, you acted like Special Forces. So, what's going on?"

"I mean you no harm," he said in a low voice.

"I already know that," I said.

He nodded. "Right. What was that stuff you put in the food last night?"

I remembered how he'd looked at me when he'd first tasted the shepherd's pie. He was the only one who'd noticed anything odd, as far as I could tell.

I didn't want to tell him too much, because I didn't know who he was or how much he knew. I put my hands out to the side, palms up. "Only a little something that is supposed to help me tell friend from foe."

He leaned closer. "You've got a very powerful foe, but you know that, don't you?"

I was so glad that somebody else seemed to know about Athu-ba. At least, I hoped that's what he was referring to. "What do you know about it?"

He took a sip of his beer. It was still three quarters full; he'd been drinking as sparingly as I had. "It's a bit of a long story. I guess I'm going to trust you."

I nodded. "I'll trust you, too."

"Okay. All cards on the table. I didn't meet Logan at the Glastonbury Music Festival. I visited with his coven, looking for information."

"Coven? So you're a—"

"Wizard. Yeah."

I digested that for a moment, though I suppose I'd had my suspicions since he'd looked at me oddly after ingesting magic potion. "And Logan?"

He nodded. "And Logan."

I may not be great at math, but even I could figure out that three people being witches at a dinner party of nine was against the odds and highly unlikely to be coincidence. "Were you working together?"

"No. He really couldn't remember where he'd met me, or he never would've mentioned it. I gave him a hard time about that afterwards." He looked down at his plate. "Now, I wish I hadn't."

"Do you have any idea how he really died?" I leaned even closer. "Was he murdered?" I'd been hanging onto hope that he might have been one of those unlucky young people who do drop dead of natural causes.

"I think we have to assume he was killed by the same character who wants to kill you."

I'd been warned by the mirror, but he hadn't. "How do you know someone wants to kill me?"

His jaw went rigid and once more I saw an angry, dangerous man. "I've been tracking that murderous swine for a couple of years now. He murdered my mentor, a wonderful, wise woman, who was the heart of our community. I wasn't able to save her, but right before she died, she said she feared he was headed to Glastonbury next. When I got there, it was too late. Did you read about the mysterious death of the occult leader? They made it sound like the guy was barmy and took his own life, but that wasn't true. Then, a powerful psychic got a vision of your mother in Egypt."

"My mother," I said.

"I needed to get close to Dr. Susan Bartlett-Swift, see if she was somehow connected."

"So, you pretended to be an archaeologist?"

"I'm an archaeologist, that part's true, but I still needed to pull some strings to get a place here. My plan was to head over to Egypt and volunteer. I thought that if I just showed up, and didn't care about getting paid, they wouldn't bother to send me away. But, then I heard that your parents were coming here."

"So you came to Oxford, deliberately to meet my parents."

"That's right. So did Logan, though we didn't know we were on the same errand at first. Logan wasn't an archaeology student at all; he used magic to get his accreditation. I wonder if that's how the demon picked up on him?"

"So Logan was trying to avenge someone's death?"

"That's right. The occult leader was his stepfather, the one who taught him. The weird thing was, we both thought your mother was the target. But, no offense to your mum, but you don't have to be around her for long to realize she's many things, but not a witch. It was last night, when I knew you'd put some kind of spell on that food, that I realized you were the witch in the family. You must be the real target."

I pushed my plate to the side. "My mother has witch blood in her, she's just deeply convinced in the rational and refuses to accept that part of herself."

"Does she know about you?"

I laughed. "She gave me a lecture, just the other day, telling me there's no such thing as ghosts, or witches, or goblins."

"It's an awful thing, having a parent who won't recognize who you really are."

I rubbed at a scatter of salt on the table top. "They love me, and they did their best."

"But you can't expect any help there. Lucy, you can't fight this thing alone, who else do you have?"

I thought of the three vampires even now watching us. I didn't share that with Pete, though, I suspected he might not be as tolerant of vampires as I had learned to be. I said, "I got some help, and a magical spell, from a powerful witch who lives near Oxford." I felt annoyed every time I thought about how she'd taken Nyx from me. "But she didn't give me the spell for free, she made me pay for it."

He didn't look all that surprised. "Sometimes, that makes

the magic more powerful. Especially if the price is a high one."

Then the spell ought to be very powerful.

Pete popped another french fry, laden with blood-red ketchup, into his mouth. I, however, had lost my appetite. "So, poor Logan died trying to save me."

His eyes grew serious. More serious than I had ever seen them. "No, Lucy. He died trying to avenge the death of his stepfather. You are not responsible for any of this."

Then why did I feel like crap?

Even though the pub was filled to capacity and noisy I still leaned closer and dropped my tone. "Has it occurred to you, that you are in danger, too?"

That, *no worries, mate, she'll be right*, attitude had completely disappeared and I saw in front of me a much more serious man. He said, "Yes. Of course, it's occurred to me."

I'd been thinking. I said, "I don't even think you should stay in the college dorm. If they got to Logan, they can get to you."

"And what do you propose I do? Run away?" He shook his head. "Not an option."

"What about staying with the powerful witch? Margaret Twig? I don't like her, but at least you'd be safe there."

"And miles away from you. No. Remember, we're more powerful together than we are individually. And, we have a slight advantage of knowing that he's coming."

A couple came and stood too close. I reached for my bag and Pete half rose, but it was only a couple of tourists come to look at the photos.

"Look, Ed. That's Tolkien, right there. And the man in

that picture over there is C.S. Lewis. I don't know who the other fellows are, but they were known as the Inklings. Imagine, dreaming up dwarf books while sitting in a pub. Some folks have all the luck." They moved on, then, carrying their full glasses, looking for a place to sit.

I said, "But the demon knows we know. Logan wasn't a powerful wizard, so why kill him? I think he's toying with us, trying to scare us."

"I don't think he knows about me," Pete mused. "That's one card we still have up our sleeves."

I wasn't certain. This evil thing, whatever it was, seemed vastly powerful to me.

I felt as though I were being constantly watched, and that it was just biding its time. The tension of waiting, and wondering when the attack would come, was getting to me. I said, still keeping my voice low, "Do you know anything about Logan's death? Anything that might help us?"

He shook his head. "I didn't even hear about it until his body had already been moved. I managed to magic my way into his room, but there was nothing there. His belongings looked undisturbed."

"Had his bed been slept in?" I asked.

He narrowed his eyes, and I could tell he was concentrating. He shook his head. "No. The bed was still made."

"Have you talked to Priya?"

He shook his head. "I didn't know what to say."

"You have her contact information?"

He pulled out his phone. "Yeah."

"Logan left my flat with Priya. Maybe she saw or heard something."

He nodded. "I'll text her right now."

He sent out the text and we both pushed our half-eaten plates of food to the edge of the table. "I'll get us some coffees," I said. Before he could protest that he would get them, I was already standing. I headed to the bar, which had a crowd around it, big enough that I could stand beside Rafe without it looking remarkable. Knowing he had excellent hearing, I spoke just above a whisper. I let him know that Pete was one of my kind, and that we were going to try and visit Priya.

He said, "I think you should go straight home. There's a funny energy about, tonight."

CHAPTER 15

I turned to stare at him, forgetting all about my intention to look as though we were complete strangers who happened to be standing at the same bar. "I thought it was just me being strung out. I feel it, too."

Rafe glanced over my head, and scanned the bar, much as Pete had been doing all evening. "I think he's going to strike, and strike soon. He's already managed to get into a college and kill. I don't want you anywhere near there. It's too hard to keep you safe."

"But, Priya might know something. Anything that might help us defeat this evil can only add to our weaponry."

I knew he was about to argue further, but at that moment Pete walked up to me and said, "Forget the coffee. I've heard from our friend. She wants to meet up."

He cast a curious, and what I considered rather male and possessive, glance at Rafe, and then we left.

Once we were outside, in the comparative quiet of Giles Street, he said, "Who was that bloke?"

"What bloke?"

He stopped walking and turned, putting his hands on my shoulders and holding me still. "Don't play games with me. That bloke you were talking to in the pub. You two were eyeing each other all night."

If I had doubted he had the extrasensory abilities of a wizard, I no longer did. I said, "He's a friend. We can trust him."

Pete's eyes were hard on mine. "He's not a wizard."

"No. He's not."

"Then what's his deal?"

I hesitated, but I had no right to tell a comparative stranger that he just been sharing the pub with vampires. Perhaps, after so many centuries of being distrusted by humans, witches were equally distrustful of other beings they didn't understand. I couldn't risk him spreading the word about our local vampires and putting them at risk. So, all I said was, "He's an expert in ancient manuscripts." And then, I sighed, realizing I was going to have to tell him more if I was going to trust him to help me.

I'd been keeping the existence of the mirror to myself, but he was right, I couldn't fight this thing on my own. So I told Pete about the mirror, how my mother had been impelled to bring it to me, and that I had asked Rafe for his opinion, both on the age of the item and the meaning of the ancient Egyptian words. I was, in fact, completely truthful. I just kept back one salient fact. That Rafe was a vampire.

Pete asked, "Where is this mirror?"

This time, I did tell a lie. On one level I felt I could trust him, but on another I was cautious. "I left it at home."

I don't know whether he believed me or not. "Priya said

she'd meet us at the coffee shop on the corner. I think she's too frightened to go far."

"I don't blame her."

We walked the rest of the way in silence, both of us no longer having to pretend that we weren't extra vigilant. My ears weren't as sharp as Rafe's, but my hearing was fairly acute. Every footfall, every cough or low conversation, had me turning to spot the source. But the only people out tonight were tourists, a giggling bunch of drunk women in heels celebrating a hen party, and students.

When we arrived at the coffee shop, we paused at the window to look inside. Being so near one of the colleges, most of the tables were packed with students sitting in front of open laptops, some with notebooks or textbooks beside them. Priya was near the back, staring at an open laptop. Though her fingers were moving on the keys, it didn't look as though her attention was engaged by the screen. I thought she only had the computer open to give her something to focus on. Her face looked drawn, and exhausted.

No one else in the coffee shop looked remotely suspicious or interested in us as we walked in. Only Priya glanced up and put up a hand and half waved.

We walked over and she stood, rather awkwardly, as we approached. I didn't know her very well, but I went with my instincts and pulled her into my arms for a hug. She clung for a moment and I could feel that she needed the support. After that, Pete also hugged her and then we sat down.

A bearded server wearing a T-shirt that advertised a rowing meet came over and Pete and I both ordered coffee while Priya went with chamomile tea. She was clearly looking for something that would help her sleep or at least not keep her awake.

When the server had left, and it was just three of us, I said, "Priya, I am so sorry about Logan."

She nodded and blinked rapidly, but she couldn't stop the tears welling in her eyes. "I can't believe it. He was fine when we walked back from your place. He'd had a bit too much to drink, but he wasn't drunk or anything. He was joking and so looking forward to going on the dig. And then, this morning, he was dead.

"I don't know what I'm going to do." She put her head in her hands. "The police said I was the last person to see him alive. Why does that make me feel so guilty?" She glanced up as though we knew the answer.

I said, "I feel guilty, too. Because he ate his last meal in my flat."

"He wanted me to stay the night, and I refused." She began to weep. "Maybe if I'd stayed, he'd be all right. I'd have heard him choking, or noticed that he was in trouble, and been able to call for help. I'm even trained in first aid."

Pete and I exchanged glances. How could we tell her we didn't think she had been the last person to see him alive? That distinction belonged to his killer.

Pete reached over and took one of her hands in his. "If he went that fast, there was probably nothing you could have done."

She sniffed and used one of the napkins from the dispenser on the table to blow her nose. "That's what the police said."

"The police?" Pete asked, as though surprised they'd interviewed her.

She nodded, "Because it was such a sudden death and he was so young, and because I was the one who found him." She dissolved into tears again. Pete was doing an excellent job of gently interrogating her and so I left him to it, trying to open up my other senses to hear what she wasn't saying.

Her whole body looked tense and miserable. Completely consistent with shock and grief. She could be acting, of course, but she'd also passed the shepherd's pie test.

"What did the police want to know?" Pete asked.

I got the feeling that she was grateful someone was asking her these questions, and giving her a chance to talk through her terrible experience. It was also clear that she and Pete, along with Logan, had become quite friendly. I could tell that she trusted him.

She took another napkin and wiped her eyes. "They asked me how I found him. We'd agreed to meet up for breakfast. He didn't come to my room like he'd said he would, but I imagined he was hung over or sleeping in, so I went to rouse him. His door was locked and when I banged on it there was no answer. I started to get a bad feeling. I got the porter to let me in." She looked sheepish. "I had to say I was his girlfriend."

Pete glanced at me and I nodded imperceptibly. He was doing a great job getting the story out of her on his own. I thought the best thing I could do was stay quiet.

"When the porter opened the door, Logan was lying on the floor. I thought at first he'd fallen out of bed, or passed out or something. We called his name and I shook his arm and then he fell onto his back and his eyes were still open. I think I knew right away, but I checked his pulse to be certain. And then the porter called 999."

"What was he wearing?" Pete asked.

Good, it was the question in my mind. I wasn't sure if Pete was able to pick up my questions, if I concentrated on them hard enough, or whether he was following the same train of thought I was.

She looked startled by the question. "The police asked me that, too. He was fully dressed. Wearing the same clothes he'd worn to dinner at your place," she said, glancing at me.

"So he hadn't been to bed?"

"I don't know. He could've gotten up early and dressed in the same clothes he'd been wearing the night before." She glanced at Pete. "He did that a lot."

"Did you notice anything strange?" Pete asked. "Out of the ordinary?"

"You mean, apart from a twenty-four-year-old university student being dead on the floor?"

"Sorry, yeah, apart from that."

"The porter asked if he'd been smoking. Obviously, there's no smoking allowed in the dorm rooms, and anyway, Logan didn't smoke." She looked at Pete, "Did he?"

"Not that I ever saw."

"I'm positive he didn't. But the porter was right, there was a slight smell of smoke in the air. And a burn mark on the floor."

The hairs on my neck were standing up so hard they felt like porcupine spines. "A burn mark?" I asked. "You mean like a cigarette burn?"

The wonderful thing about dealing with archaeologists is how precise they are. They are trained to differentiate between, say, petrified wood and charcoal, the marks from smoke versus the marks from actual flames. I imagined she was pulling the mental picture up and trying to decide exactly what it looked like.

She said, "It wasn't from a cigarette. In fact, it wasn't a burn so much as a scorch. If you dropped a burning piece of paper onto a wooden floor, say, and it burned itself out. The burn mark had a funny shape, too, like a star."

The server returned with our drinks and we took a break while we added sugars and creams and stirred our drinks. I sipped the hot liquid in the thick-rimmed ceramic mug and thought of star-shaped scorch marks.

"Was it the same porter who let you in, when you got home last night?" Pete asked.

"No, it was a different one. Which is weird, because the porter this morning said he'd been on duty, then. He can't figure out who let us in."

I sent Pete an intense look and he asked, "Did the porter go on a break? Or fall asleep?"

"You sound just like the police. He says not, but, of course, he might have."

Pete said, possibly still reading my mind, "What did he look like, the porter from last night?"

She shrugged. "Like a porter. He was probably in his fifties. A middle-aged balding, white man. There was nothing remarkable about him. I'd say he was average height and average build, wearing a porter's uniform. I couldn't pick him out of a crowd."

I couldn't think of any more questions and I don't think Pete could, either.

We sipped our coffees until Pete asked what her plans were. "Are you still going to come on the dig with us?"

She shook her head. "Honestly, I don't know. This has been such a shock."

"And you two were close, weren't you?"

Her eyes filled with tears again. "Yeah. We were really excited about doing the dig together. I'm not sure I can do it alone."

"Well, don't make any decisions now. Give yourself a few days to recover."

She glanced at her watch. "I need to call my parents. I just need to talk to someone who loves me."

Pete said, "Come on. Lucy and I will walk you back and make sure you're locked into your room, safely."

She looked pathetically grateful to have been offered the escort. And I liked Pete the more for offering it. As we walked back, she told him that Logan's parents were already in Oxford. They'd identified the body and, as soon as it was released, they were taking Logan back to Glastonbury to be buried.

I felt such sorrow for this bright young man, gone before his time. I was determined to fight this thing with everything I had, not only for myself, and that poor trapped witch who'd been stuck in the mirror for all those years, but also for Logan.

Once we'd seen Priya settled safely in her room, Pete and I headed back to Harrington Street. He asked, "What do you reckon? Was it the porter?"

"You mean the fake porter? It had to be. That seems to be this thing's genius, it can shapeshift into something completely benign, like a university porter."

I thought again about that older man who had applied for the job as my assistant. Ned Cruikshank was exactly like that porter. A middle-aged man, no distinguishing features, average height, average build. The only thing remarkable about him had been his wool allergy. I could imagine a demon masquerading as a mild-mannered recent retiree, but why add in a wool allergy? It didn't make sense.

Mr. Cruikshank had also drunk the revealing potion with no effect. Frankly, I was beginning to wonder if the potion was any good. What if, in exchange for my beloved cat, Margaret had given me a jar of water with a few herbs boiled in it? If so, she'd put me more at risk than I was before.

"You're deep in thought," Pete said, beside me.

"Sorry. I just feel so confused. I don't know where to turn. I can't sit around waiting for this terrible evil thing to attack me. There must be a way we can go after it."

"I'm listening."

I was thinking. I stopped walking and turned to him. "What does it live on? It sounded as though there wasn't a mark on poor Logan." I was thinking, of course, of the vampires and how it was quite obvious that they'd fed off their victims because they sucked the blood out of their bodies. Meritamun had said the evil thing sucked the power and life spirit out of witches. But how? Was it something to do with those scorch marks?

"I'm going to introduce you to the only witch who actually knows him. Her name is Meritamun and, well, you'll see."

Glancing quickly up and down the street to make certain we were alone, I pulled the mirror out of my bag. Even as I touched the handle I felt that it was already warm. When I eased it out of the bag, I gave a gasp. It was already pulsing with blue light and I hadn't recited the spell.

Pete's eyes widened, his face taking on a bluish cast in the reflection of the strange light pulsing out of the mirror. "Well, I'll be damned," he said.

I felt quite panicked. "I've never seen it do this before. Always, in the past, I've had to recite that incantation in order to bring it to life. What do you think this means?"

He looked at me, completely baffled. "I don't know. I've never seen that mirror before. It looks ancient."

Right, I wasn't thinking clearly. I briefly explained the history of the mirror, as I knew it. I couldn't take a chance we'd be seen by someone out for an evening stroll, so I pulled Pete behind the wall of Jesus College, and wedged us behind a tree where hopefully, we'd be out of sight. I didn't know what to do and was glad to have a wizard to discuss this with.

"Do you think, if I recite the incantation, now, she'll still appear."

He looked dubious. "If that thing's already going off on its own, I wouldn't want to activate any more magic. Maybe he uses this Meritamun character as another lure, and if you read out those words, it won't be some sweet young Egyptian girl you conjure, it'll be the scariest monster you've ever seen come flying out of that mirror and attack you."

"So that's a no then," I said. Sarcasm was my last defense when I'm terrified.

CHAPTER 16

*P*ete couldn't take his gaze off the pulsing blue light coming out of the ancient mirror. "If I get a vote, then I say 'no.'"

I heard footsteps coming toward us and quickly pushed the mirror back into the bag, still holding onto the handle in case I needed it. I turned, ready to attack. Pete was equally vigilant, and turned at the very same moment. The footsteps slowed as they neared us, and then Alfred and Christopher Weaver walked, slowly by, glancing our way and then continuing as though they were just two old friends returning home after a night in the pub.

I put my guard down, with a small sigh of relief. Pete watched the two for a moment longer, before doing the same. We could hear snatches of their conversation as they went by. Something about rival football teams and a playoff. I suspected their entire conversation was fictitious, but they did it well. I supposed those who were different and trying to blend in in society got very good at acting a part.

Still, I didn't relax. Why was the mirror still warm in my

hand? I was certain that if I glanced into the leather bag I would see the blue light still pulsing. Was it trying to tell me something? Or was Pete right and the mirror was, in itself, a threat?

We came back onto the quiet road and kept walking. The two vampires had disappeared, but I knew they weren't far. As Pete and I walked down Harrington, toward the block where my shop was located, I think both of us became even more vigilant. An odd-looking person stood, looking in the window of the gift shop, two doors down from Cardinal Woolsey's. It was a woman, and something about the posture looked vaguely familiar. She wore a long, black garment that looked almost like a cloak. A large hood tipped over her head so it shadowed her face. She was carrying a covered basket, rather like Little Red Riding Hood had except with a black cape. As we grew closer, I could hear strange sounds coming from the basket.

It sounded as though a wild animal were trapped in there. It was snarling, and spitting, and then meowing. I sped up, thinking I recognized that meow.

"What's going on?" Pete asked me in a whisper, lengthening his stride to keep up with me. I was walking so fast I was nearly at a jog. "I think that's my cat."

Oh, please let it be Nyx. As though the cat could sense my approach, it began to meow louder and more plaintively. At the sound of our hurrying feet, the black-cloaked figure turned our way. But whoever was holding the basket didn't move or speak until I was very close.

"Margaret?" I asked. The figure was the right size and general shape, but why on earth was she hiding her face?

"Be careful," Pete warned, and I knew he was right. I

should be very wary, considering that I had no way of identifying the cat and the figure hadn't shown itself.

The mirror was getting warmer in my hand.

My heart was thumping, but I think it was partly in anticipation of hopefully being reunited with Nyx as well as nervous excitement caused by the strange actions of the mirror.

I slowed down and began to approach more slowly. And then the figure pushed the basket out toward me and said in a voice that I definitely recognized as Margaret's, "Is that you, Lucy? Take this bloody cat and don't let it come near me, ever again."

She unclasped the wicker basket and opened the lid and Nyx leapt out and right into my arms.

"Nyx," I cried cradling my cat in my arms. Already I began to feel better. Nyx was an important part of my team, and I couldn't go into battle without her.

I was curious, though, as to why Margaret had demanded her as payment and now seemed so annoyed to have had the keeping of her.

Margaret made a sound, rather like Nyx when she was spitting mad in the basket. "Oh, now she's purring! Look at that creature, cuddled up against you as though she's the sweetest tempered cat in the world. Well, you'd better have a spell to cure this, or I will hex you."

After spitting out those enraged words, she eased her hood back and, with an astonished gasp, I realized why she was so annoyed. Her face was liberally streaked with scratches and each one of them had erupted into a string of horrible looking boils and warts. My favorite was the particularly bulbous wart on the end of her slightly pointed nose. I tickled Nyx under the chin, one of her favorite spots, to let her know how deeply I approved of her actions.

I wanted to tell Margaret Twig that perhaps this would be a lesson to her not to steal another witch's familiar, but I had to bear in mind that she was not only a very powerful witch, but she'd given me the revealing potion, assuming it worked, and helped me with the spell.

I tried to be sympathetic. "I'll look in my family grimoire. I must have some kind of spell that will work."

Then I looked at her again. "But you're a much more powerful witch than I am. Couldn't you cure yourself?"

She pointed a finger at Nyx and I saw that it was so covered in warts and boils, she couldn't straighten it. Her finger was hooked and hideous looking. "That little varmint is more powerful than I am. In fact, I think it's the devil itself."

Nothing could look less like the devil than the sweet, black cat purring contentedly in my arms. She was sleek, and warm, still halfway between kitten and cat. I said, "Nyx, you're home now. Can you help me cure Margaret? She promises she'll never take you again."

The cat half-closed its green eyes and I swear it was glaring at Margaret. Then, Nyx turned to me and licked my hand with her sandpaper tongue. As she was looking at me, I suddenly knew exactly what I had to do. I recited the words of a simple spell for the cure of skin ailments that I'd found in my grimoire.

It had worked when I'd thrown out a truly annoying pimple. Maybe it would work on a curse of boils and warts. I wasn't sure I remembered the words exactly, but I'd found with magic a lot of the power was in the intent and the way I concentrated. I looked at Margaret's truly messed up face and, after letting myself enjoy the sight for one more second, pulled all my focus into picturing smooth skin on her face and hands.

This imperfection is painful to see,
Smooth of skin, let her be.
So I say, so mote it be.

As I said the simple rhyme, I reached forward and touched my fingers, still damp from where Nyx had licked them, against the marks on Margaret's face.

Immediately they disappeared. All that was left was the faintest scratches which grew fainter as I watched. It was like magic!

"Now her hands," I said to Nyx, sounding firm, but stroking her belly with my other hand so she'd know it was just for show. Nyx obediently licked my hand again and I touched both Margaret's hands.

"That should take care of it," I said.

I wasn't certain she believed me but she reached into a rather capacious handbag and withdrew a compact mirror, which she used to look her face. She tilted her face this way and that and then pulled the hood away from her head. She didn't look very grateful. "There are still scratches on my face."

I thought 'thank you' might've been a more appropriate response, but then I hadn't lived with warts and boils all over my face and hands for several days. I looked closely at her.

"They're fading minute by minute. If they're not completely gone by tomorrow, come back and I'll do another treatment."

She sniffed, clearly annoyed at receiving instructions from a much younger and less experienced witch, but, she had to know, as I did, that the magic was coming, not from me, but from Nyx. Finally, glaring at the cat, she nodded.

Then, almost as though seeing Pete for the first time, she snapped, "And you'd better do a forgetting spell on that one."

"He's one of us," I said.

Pete nodded. "Margaret Twig. You came to Sydney to give a workshop on healing herbs. Very impressive it was, too. I think we all learned a lot that evening."

I got the feeling that Margaret's evening was suddenly improving. She looked at Pete and then dipped her chin and flirted with her eyes. "Thank you. You've got some very accomplished witches down your way."

Now that she'd calmed down and I had my cat back, I felt more kindly disposed to Margaret. Also, I was curious as to whether she had felt the odd change in energy in the atmosphere. "Have you been aware of a strange energy this evening?"

She looked at me, sharply. "I thought it was just my own anger reflecting back at me because of what that wretched cat did to my face."

"Are you still feeling it?"

She breathed in and out, slowly, and closed her eyes. I had Nyx back and was within a few feet of my home, where I felt safe, and yet, I was still aware of the scent of danger, the crackle of negative energy in the air. It was hard to explain, like a faint scent that you grow accustomed to, but if you stop to smell it, you find it's there.

She opened her eyes and nodded. "There is something." She looked at me closely. "You're not dead, I see. But I take it you haven't vanquished the demon who's after you. The revealing potion didn't work?"

"Well, it hasn't revealed a monster, if that's what you mean. But I've trusted that if someone consumed it and didn't turn into something nasty, that they were probably safe."

She shrugged. "Unless the evil one is powerful enough to neutralize the spell."

Now she told me this was a possibility? I felt like scratching her myself and cursing her with a fresh dose of boils and warts. "You mean, it might not work?"

Her cloak fluttered as she shrugged her shoulders. "It's a very faint possibility."

I'd had enough of this witch and her condescending attitude. "I'm going inside, now. My mother's been alone all evening and, knowing her, she probably forgot to eat. I'd invite you in, but Mom doesn't believe in witches."

"Good heavens. Witch blood runs through her, strong and true, it's very sad to deny one's true nature."

People kept saying this, but I wasn't so sure. "I really don't think Mom's a witch."

"Nonsense. That's why your magic is so powerful. She's denied her own, and it had to go somewhere, so it came to you."

I didn't really like the sound of that. "You mean I'm like a double witch?"

Pete said, "You're a super witch, you've been supersized."

I shook my head at both of them. "You two have a lovely evening, I'm going home to bed, now."

"Wait," Pete said. "I'm coming in with you. I want to make sure everything's okay, and then I'll go back home." He shot a cheeky look at Margaret. "Your mum likes me."

I had Nyx now, so I didn't really need him, but he'd been so kind to me that I didn't have the heart to tell him he couldn't come in. I nodded and began walking towards my shop.

"Wait," Margaret said, scurrying to catch up with us. "With that funny energy in the air, I think you need all the help you can get. I'm coming too."

"Fine," I said again. "But, remember, you're just a friend I've met in Oxford."

"You can tell her I'm your cat sitter," she said, and reached out to pat Nyx's head. Nyx hissed and took a swipe at her, claws extended.

"Yep, she'll believe that one."

CHAPTER 17

We got to the knitting shop and, though the blind was closed, I could see a faint light inside. I'd have gone all the way around and into the house from the back way, but since I'd obviously left a lamp burning, I decided to go in through the shop.

I unlocked the door and, as I did, I noticed something really strange was going on with the mirror in my bag. It began to hum. I glanced at the others to see if they could hear it, but they were talking about mutual acquaintances in Australia. I glanced up and down the dark street again. I'd be so glad when I was safely inside, spending what was left of the evening with my mother, knowing I had loads of protectors near me. While I knew the vampires could be trusted around most humans, I suspected that they'd be only too pleased to let their instincts to kill and destroy take over if there was a genuine monster to be beaten.

I opened the shop door and went inside. To my surprise, my assistant was sitting in the chair, rapidly crocheting one of her small dolls. She was wearing a purple coat dress that set off the silver gray of her hair. Her pink lipstick was freshly applied. In fact, she looked as though she were ready for the workday to begin, when it was nearly bedtime.

"Eileen," I said, in surprise.

She stood up and smiled at me. "Good evening, Lucy. You're rather late home. Out whoring, I imagine. Your mother was getting worried."

Whoring? Had I heard her correctly?" As I stared, wondering whether to chastise her for criticizing my personal behavior, or ask her why she was here, I noticed something very peculiar. Her outline began to shimmer.

The humming of the mirror grew louder and I gripped the mirror tighter in my hand. *Oh, no!* Not Eileen. Not my trusted assistant. But I didn't like the look in her eyes, or that she'd referred to Mom. "What do you mean, my mother's worried about me?"

My heart was pounding uncomfortably fast and I was so happy to have Pete and Margaret as backup.

Nyx made a sound I'd never heard her make before. She was growling, deep in her throat. Almost in tune with that humming coming from the mirror.

Then, from the back room, I heard a voice that was unmistakably my mother's. She called out, "Lucy, run!"

I glanced behind me, to the still open door, not so I could run, but to make sure that Pete and Margaret were behind me. I was so happy they had decided to come in with me, as I felt certain I was about to need all the help I could get. But, to my horror, I could see them both on the other side of the shop's doorway. Their mouths were open and it seemed as though they were speaking, or, more likely, yelling, and banging their fists on what looked to be nothing but air.

Eileen said, still in that comfortable, grandmotherly tone, "I think it's time your friends went home."

And then, waving her crochet hook like a wand, and muttering something in a language I had never heard, she caused the door to bang shut in their faces.

No doubt Margaret had a spell that was equally powerful. I had to trust that she and Pete would break through the barrier, but, in the meantime, I needed to find out what was going on with my mother.

I started toward the back and Eileen didn't stop me. In fact, she followed along, her orthopedic shoes making soft, tapping sounds on the wood floor.

I pulled back the curtain and there was Mom.

She was sitting on one of the chairs in the back room. She was still dressed in the same black slacks and blue sweater that she'd been wearing earlier. She looked for all the world like one of the vampire knitters who'd shown up early. Except that her arms appeared to be fastened behind her back and she was unable to rise out of the chair. Now that I looked, I could see her ankles were tied to the chair legs with coarse rope. She was also tied at the waist. Her eyes looked glassy with shock.

"Mom!" I cried, running towards her. I put Nyx down so my hands were free to untie her. But, before I was close enough to touch her, a burst of fire exploded in my path. It was so shocking, and so unexpected, that I screamed and jumped back. This was no pyrotechnic illusion of fake flame. I felt the heat and, to my shock, heard the crackle and pop as the wooden floor of my shop caught fire. I could see Mom, on the other side of the wall of flames, struggling in her chair. I was terrified she'd knock it over and the wooden chair would catch fire.

I didn't know the spell to turn out a fire, I was only a baby, fledgling witch, but my mother was on the other side of that flame. I needed to focus. That was all I could think of. I remembered my grandmother telling me that a witch's strength came from the natural world, from the elements, and being able to use their strength as hers. I imagined that I was cool water. I pictured a waterfall. We'd taken a family trip up to Maine one summer, I remembered. Mom and Dad and me. We'd taken a walk and a picnic one day, to a waterfall. It wasn't particularly spectacular, as waterfalls go, but I could remember my parents holding hands, looking so happy, and the way I'd felt out in nature. I drew on all of that. The love and support of people I cared about, the feeling of being one with nature, and then I focused all my attention on the memory of that waterfall. I started to feel chilly, as I did when one of the vampires touched me.

I said aloud, "Put the fire out." It wasn't any kind of a spell, there was no rhyme, no magic incantation, but no words uttered by any witch could have been more sincere.

I looked over at Nyx, who obligingly came near, and I picked up the cat and held her, picturing the waterfall dumping water on the fire. The fire dimmed, and the flames dropped until they were only rising about two or three inches above the ground, but they were still burning.

I said, again, holding Nyx's small, warm body against mine, both of us now looking at the flames. "Put the fire out."

And, then, as though the flame had been turned off, it simply went out.

I put the cat down and once more ran towards my mother.

As my foot hit the ashy place where the fire had been, pain shot through my foot and up my leg. I let out a scream and fell back. I'd never touched an electric fence, but I knew instinctively that's what she'd done. She'd erected an invisible electric fence between me and Mom.

I turned my head, and there was Eileen, standing in the doorway, resting her hands on her ample belly. She shook her head. "Use your intelligence, dear. I'm not going to let you cross that circle."

"There's no need to harm my mother. She is not a witch."

The creature, for I could no longer even think of it as Eileen, my-oh-so-helpful assistant, pulled another of the wooden chairs toward her and sat comfortably on it, resuming her crochet. She was between me and the doorway back to the front of the shop.

"Of course, your mother's a witch. She's deeply in denial. But, once you're gone, who's to say she won't suddenly embrace her inner powers? And the desire for revenge is a powerful force. No, it would be too tedious to have to come back and dispose of another one of you. Besides, I think it will be rather amusing to let you watch your mother die."

She was sewing a couple of button eyes onto one of her crocheted dolls. While she appeared to be concentrating on her handiwork, I pulled the mirror from out of my bag and, pointing it toward her, began to recite the spell Margaret had given me. Eileen didn't look up from her work.

I'd only got a few words out when she took the needle she was using to sew on the buttons and very calmly stabbed it into the wrist of the doll. I screamed, feeling the terrible pain go through my own wrist, and the mirror clattered to the floor. As I looked down, I could see blood trickling out of my wrist, exactly as though a pin had stabbed me there.

"You are becoming a bore." The creature might sound casual, but I imagined a great deal of energy was being expended in order to maintain the perimeter barrier that was keeping out Margaret and Pete. Then it had caused the fire and stabbed me. I noticed that the creature was having trouble sustaining the Eileen image. Not only was it still wavering around the edges, but Eileen's face was beginning to change, twisting out of shape.

Whatever was underneath, it was horrific. I caught a glimpse of something skeletal, and hollow-eyed, with flames leaping up into the empty sockets. The creature seemed to shake itself back into the Eileen persona, but I wondered how much energy it was taking to keep all the strong spells going at once. Enough to weaken it, I hoped.

Margaret would be pushing, just as hard as she could, to break that spell keeping her out, I knew. Pete was no doubt helping, although, from the sounds of banging, I suspected he was more interested in human, physical force, at the moment. He was leaving the magic to Margaret.

No doubt the creature intended to suck the energy out of me and Mom and refill its tank. I did not intend to let that happen. I wasn't sure I could do it alone, though.

Where was Rafe? And the other vampires? They must've heard the screams.

I noticed that the trapdoor was latched from my side. What if I could open it? What if that perimeter spell only worked around the edges of my shop and home, not above or below?

I looked over at Nyx, the only magical creature who was

both inside, and my ally. The cat had retreated and jumped up onto the table where we kept the tea things. She was lying, Sphinx like, with her paws forward and her head up. In that moment, and in that pose, she looked as regal and as dangerous as a cat goddess. She seemed to be biding her time. What else could she do?

My mother still looked glassy-eyed with shock, but otherwise seemed unharmed. I thought, perhaps, she'd seen glimpses of the creature and simple horror kept her frozen, sitting in that chair. She wasn't even struggling against her bonds. Almost as though she accepted she was about to be sacrificed, and was determined to go with dignity.

But I wasn't going with dignity, and I wasn't letting my mother go, either. Not without every drop of fight I could summon.

Seeing Nyx sitting beside the tea things had given me an idea. I said, "Eileen, why don't I make us a nice cup of tea, and we can talk about this?"

The creature looked completely like Eileen again. Her voice was as sweet as always. "If you like, dear. There's no hurry. I can't leave until your father gets home."

Oh my God, not my dad. "Leave him out of this," I said. "He's completely mortal, you must know that."

"Of course, I do. But I don't want loose ends. There's going to be a very tragic house fire, I'm sorry to say. With all this wool and these paper patterns, and the old timbers at the heart of the house, it will be a real conflagration." She said the word with relish. "There'll be no sign of foul play. Just another, tragic accident. They do happen, every day."

I felt frantic, now. If only I could think clearly. I had to keep control of my emotions. I needed to conserve my energy, and my power, and think. She let me put the kettle on and I clattered the cups together so she'd think my hands were shaking. In fact, they were remarkably steady. I could feel a cold stillness inside me. I can't explain it, but I suddenly felt I was drawing power from other sources than simply myself.

I looked at my mother. She was staring at me with the most curious expression on her face and I thought—no, I realized— that she was, at that moment, embracing her power as a witch, and, I suspect, freeing it. I closed my eyes and let our powers join. Nyx butted her head against my knuckles, where I was leaning against the table and, yes, I felt her power, too. And I felt it coming from Margaret, and Pete, and whatever network they were drawing from. All the witches past and present of Oxford seemed to whisper to me, *You are not alone.*

The water had begun to boil. I slipped the bottle of revealing potion from my bag. I didn't bother to make it into tea, I poured the liquid straight into the tea mug, and covered it with boiling water. Then, walking over as though to offer Eileen a cup of tea, I threw the liquid over her.

She jumped and twisted, crying out, but more in rage than pain. And, then, I almost wished I hadn't splashed the revealing potion on her, because it was powerful. In horror I watched, as the Eileen façade fell away, following the splash pattern of the revealing spell. One arm was still clad in its purple coat dress, and part of her chest remained in the form I'd known as Eileen. Most of the face and hair remained, but what was beneath it was like a living skeleton pulsing with fire and the most horrible, sickly substance that looked liquid.

The evil thing glared at me. "That wasn't very wise."

"Go away from here, and leave us alone." I sounded like a scared teenager in a horror film. That's pretty much how I felt.

The creature, part Eileen and part monster, sneered. "Now, how shall we get rid of Mummy? I like to make the death fit the victim. That vile young wizard, Logan, was heartsick over that dull young woman, the archaeology student. When they said goodbye, he said to her, 'You make my heart want to explode.' That was a fitting end for him." The chuckle was part Eileen, and part something unearthly. The sound of evil.

"When they do the autopsy, that's what they'll find. They'll call it an aneurysm, quite common in cases of mysterious death among the young. But, really, his heart exploded. I call that poetic justice, don't you?"

She stretched out the doll she'd now finished and took another one from out of her knitting bag. I could see, now, that the second poppet had hair made out of black wool with two strands of white wool interspersed. I remembered the way she'd plunged a needle into the second doll and I had felt the pain. That doll I now realized had yellow wool stuck to its head.

"No," I whispered.

How could I have been so stupid? She'd even called them poppets in my hearing, and I'd assume she referred to poppet as a darling little creature, referring mostly to her grandchildren. Of course, poppets were also a kind of voodoo doll, a representation of a person and when you did ill to that doll, the human victim felt it.

The thing smiled at me, a ghastly sort of smile, and a

flame licked out from between its lips. "You were remarkably stupid, but finally you understand."

"I trusted you."

She chuckled again. "The perfect ending for a witch who owns a knitting shop, should be death by wool and needles, don't you agree?"

It was horrible to hear that sweet older woman's voice emerging from this half human, half horror vision thing. I wished I hadn't thrown the revealing potion on it, now, it was so hideous to look at I could hardly bear it.

I didn't say anything. I had no idea how to reach it, and suspected if I tried to reason with it, I'd only make things worse. The creature took the fingers of her still mostly-human looking hand and pulled the black and white wool, as though testing it were tight against the doll. My mother cried out, her hair sticking straight up and seeming to pull her up and out of the chair, except the rope around her waist held her down. I could see the skin of her forehead stretching, and then the creature let go and she slumped back into the chair.

The Eileen thing said, "I could simply burn the doll, but that would be so quick, and so obvious, really. She'll burn in the end, of course, but let's not be in a rush."

"There must be something I can do," I said through dry lips. "Something you want."

She chuckled again. "This is what I want." She looked at her poppet, and at me, and then at Mom. "Let's just simply unravel her. That should be fun."

Do something, I said to myself.

I got to my feet ran at the creature, thinking if I moved fast enough, I could grab the doll away from her, but I was thrown back by the electric shock before I got within three feet of her. The force threw me right against the wall, and I slid down to the floor. My feet bumped against the rug that we used to cover the trapdoor.

I could feel them down there, I was sure of it. In the corner of the room, was the basket I had brought down the very first time we'd held a vampire knitting club meeting. It still held holy water, and the wooden knitting needles, that I'd sharpened.. I doubled over and crawled, on my hands and knees, using the attack as my excuse to get close to the basket. I reached in and, to my relief, the knitting needles were still there. I picked one up.

Wands were really more like divining rods, a way of focusing the power of the spell. I said the words that would open a locked door and pointed my wand at the trapdoor. I heard the click as it opened, and then I waited.

The creature hadn't even noticed; she was too busy tormenting my mother. She had knotted the very beginning of her work, and the knot had settled under the soles of the doll's feet. "We'll begin at the bottom, and work up. That way, your mother can watch her own death. It's not everyone who can say that." And then she snipped the knot, took the loose end of wool, and began to pull.

As the stitches unravelled, Mom screamed and began to squirm.

Her feet disappeared.

CHAPTER 18

The carpet moved and then, to my great relief, Rafe and Alfred and Christopher Weaver exploded into the room. The creature rose and let out a hideous cry, as, snarling, pale, and bloodthirsty, the vampires advanced.

They cried out and fell back as they hit the electrical force field, but that moment of inattention was everything to me. I grabbed the mirror. It was pulsing with light and humming again, and as I recited the spell Margaret had given me, I felt the power fill me and course through me. I pushed through the vampires and held the mirror up in front of the creature's terrifying eyes.

"Look away!" I yelled to my friends, closing my own eyes and looking down. As the full impact of the evil clashed with its own reflection, there was a terrible explosion. I couldn't hold onto the mirror, anymore. It was ripped out of my hands. Behind my closed eyelids I could see the glow of a great fire and then it faded and I opened my eyes.

There was nothing on the ground, now, but a pile of smoldering embers. Rafe rushed forward and stamped on them, kicking the live coals apart. Pete and Margaret came running in, and Pete immediately began helping Rafe, stomping and spreading the living embers until they were nothing but dead ash.

I ran forward to my mother. I fumbled the knots with shaking fingers until Margaret, whose wits were better than mine, cast a freedom spell and immediately untied my mother.

Mom couldn't rise from the chair, though, as her feet were gone.

There was no blood or obvious damage. It was as though someone had taken an eraser to a picture of Mom and had erased her feet and one of her ankles.

I glanced at Margaret. "Can you fix that?"

"I don't know. How was it done?"

"It was the doll, where's the doll?" I looked around and saw Nyx pick up the poppet as though it were a toy. The cat glared at Margaret, walked past her, and dropped the remains of the crocheted poppet daintily at my feet. "Good cat," I said.

Margaret rolled her eyes. "No wonder she hated me. You treat that animal like it's a dog."

"Nyx is my faithful friend, whatever she is."

I stroked Nyx and she began to purr. Margaret picked up the poppet and where the knitted doll's legs ended was a long strand of wool hanging down.

Christopher Weaver stepped forward and held out his hand. "Allow me." He took the doll from Margaret. Christopher Weaver wasn't only a vampire, he was a doctor and I was hopeful he might be able to heal Mom.

He rubbed the wool between his fingers and looked

closely at the size of the stitches. He looked around on the floor and found the crochet hook Eileen had used.

Then he looked over at Mom and Margaret and Pete and Rafe and Alfred. Everyone was staring at him. "Do you mind if I go into the front shop? I find all the attention unnerving."

"Of course, you don't have to ask." I bit my lip. "But please, hurry."

My mother sat there, footless, looking stunned. Margaret spoke to her in a low voice, comforting her, I think, and telling her not to worry. "We'll soon have you back on your feet."

We exchanged a glance and Margaret winced at her own presumably accidental and most unfortunate pun.

But, for some reason, the bad choice of words was the tonic my mother needed. She began to laugh. "Well," she said, "the journey of a thousand miles begins with the first step."

"Nothing like putting your best foot forward," Pete chimed in.

"Now, you've put your foot in it," Alfred said.

I couldn't stand it. I left them making terrible puns and went into the shop where I flipped on lights to make sure Christopher could see properly.

I fussed around, and waited, as he rapidly crocheted the feet back onto the doll. As he finished off the feet, and knotted the last bit of wool, a cheer went up from the back room. I sighed with relief and hugged the vampire, and then we both ran into the back where my mother was trying out her brand-new feet by standing up.

She looked down at her old running shoes. "These are very ugly shoes. What was I thinking?" She looked up and included all of us in her smile. "I will celebrate my restored feet by buying a nice new pair of shoes, tomorrow."

She walked over and wrapped me in her arms and held me tight. Her voice only shook slightly as she said, "And, I think, a pedicure. Lucy, perhaps you'll join me? I think we could both use a day at the spa."

I'd never known a woman less inclined to indulge in a day at the spa than my mother, so I knew in that moment how very much in shock she still was. Of course, I agreed.

She glanced at the pile of ash and swallowed. "If you don't mind, I think I'll go upstairs. I can't stand to be here, anymore. Please, why don't you all come up? There's half a bottle of scotch left. I think we could all use a drink."

Alfred and Christopher accompanied her upstairs, for which I was grateful. Rafe and Margaret and Pete and I remained behind. We looked down at the ashes of the former creature.

Margaret said, "We need to dispose of these remains very carefully. I must do some research. I'm not sure if it's better to scatter the ashes into the sea so they can never gather together, or bury them."

A new voice intruded. It was that of a young woman, lightly accented. I turned, and there in the darkened corner of the room, where I suppose the mirror had landed, after it flew out of my hands, was a young Egyptian woman, in a heap on the floor. I rushed over and knelt by her side, hardly believing my eyes. "Meritamun?"

She sat up shakily. The face, of course, I remembered. But, as Pete helped her to her feet, I saw that she was a young woman, about five feet tall, wearing a beautiful yellow silk robe.

I had thought the day couldn't get any more crazy. When was I going to learn never to make predictions? I had powers, but foretelling the future certainly wasn't one of them.

She put a hand to her head and said, "I'm free. I'm finally free." I looked at the golden bracelet, circling her wrist and recognized the protection spell. That must be how the evil one had originally got to her.

Margaret was both less romantic than I and more practical. She asked, "Do you know how to dispose of this creature's remains?"

"Yes. Yes. You must place the accursed ashes into an alabaster box or vessel, then take them into the desert and feed the ashes to a camel. It will be excreted in the hot sand of the desert as the camel treks. Camels go far in a single day."

"Well, that's convenient," Margaret said. "We have so many deserts around Oxford. And camels are on every street corner. I can pop into a shop and pick up an alabaster vessel."

I was shocked at her bad temper. We'd beaten Athu-ba tonight, and freed an enslaved witch. I said, "My parents will be going back to the desert soon. If we can find such a box, they can take back the ashes with them."

We all agreed that was the best thing to do and then Rafe said he owned an alabaster box. I suspected it was a priceless artifact from his collection. I told him my parents could bring it back when it was empty.

He looked down at the ashy remains and said he thought it would be best if they buried the box in the desert, too. He went home to fetch it and, while he did, Meritamun stretched out her limbs and danced around the room, laughing at the sheer joy of movement.

I was watching her, with a smile on my face, when she

suddenly stopped and came toward me and took my hands. Her eyes were downcast. "I ask your forgiveness for what I have done. My magic has been used for evil. If you wish to take my life, I willingly offer it."

I looked at Margaret, instinctively. I was too startled to speak.

Margaret said, "We don't sacrifice each other, any more. My, you've got a lot to learn." She turned to me. "The poor girl won't know about cars, planes, the Internet, and I don't know what else."

"Fast food," Pete added. "Cruise vacations. Online dating. Electricity."

She looked from one to the other, mystified. "Never mind," I said, laughing. "She'll catch up."

She put her fingers to the gold bracelet on her arm. "My father gave me this," she said sadly. "He said it would protect me, always."

Margaret walked forward and looked at the bracelet. "It wasn't his fault. Or yours. Your magic wasn't strong enough to protect yourself from Athu-ba. You've spent centuries being punished."

Meritamun nodded, looking sad. "He tricked me, and then trapped me inside the mirror."

She didn't seem able to say more, so I told Margaret what I knew. That her great usefulness to the evil one had been an uncanny ability to connect with the currently living witches who were the most powerful, and therefore the most dangerous, to Athu-ba.

Meritamun nodded. "I would see them. Like a vision. No matter how hard I tried not to. And all he had to do was look into the surface of the mirror and he would be able to see the witch in her daily life."

Pete said, "Crikey. Like an evil overlord spy cam?"

Meritamun had no idea what he was talking about. I told her I'd explain later and asked her to continue her story. She said, "And that is how it always was. I saw your mother, and then I saw you. He put a spell on the mirror so that your mother was compelled to bring it to you. He always intended to destroy both of you."

She looked at me, and the sweetness and gratitude in her face nearly undid me. She said, "Normally when anyone, even a witch, looked into that mirror, all they saw reflected was themselves. You were the only one who ever saw me."

"I wonder why?"

Margaret looked at me, sharply. "I told you that when your mother suppressed her own magic, she gave you extra powers. You must be very careful, Lucy. I suspect you are one powerful wise woman."

I didn't feel wise, I felt foolish and scared and, most days, I wished I wasn't even a witch. But there wasn't much I could do about it, now. My mother had pretended she wasn't, and that hadn't turned out so well. At least, by admitting my own abilities, I was saving my future children, if I ever had any, from turning out as much of a freak as I was.

Rafe arrived back far sooner than any mortal could have made the trip. He showed Meritamun the alabaster box. It was exquisite. Slightly greenish and carved with hieroglyphics. "Will this do?"

She took the box and opened it and then settled the lid back on again. "Yes. This is most suitable."

"But it's so gorgeous," I said. "Are you sure you don't want my parents to bring it back to you?"

He looked at me. "I'd always remember that the remains of that evil thing had been inside. No, I'll be much happier if it's buried in the desert somewhere."

He smiled slightly. "Besides, that makes room in my collection for me to acquire something new."

I retrieved the dustpan and brush and we swept up the ashes very carefully and placed them in the alabaster box. Even though the lid fitted tightly, I duct taped it shut to be certain.

Then we all went upstairs. Before I turned out the lights I glanced back and saw a curious, star-shaped scorch, so like the one in Logan's dorm room. I planned to scrub the area until the scorch mark came out or, if that didn't work, I would paint over the floor. I did not ever want to be reminded of the horrors of this evening.

When I got to the door leading up to my flat, I found that Rafe had hung back and was waiting for me. He asked, "Are you all right?"

"I think so." I rubbed my forehead with the heel of my hand. "I discovered my assistant was an evil and potent demon, nearly saw my own mother killed in front of my eyes, and discovered that she's a witch too. Yep, it's been quite an evening."

He looked at me intensely. "Being trapped down there in that passage, hearing you scream and unable to break through, it was a tough evening for me, too."

I stared at him in surprise, hearing the intensity in his tone. Our gazes connected and he placed his cool palm against my cheek. "You've become important to me, Lucy. I couldn't bear it if anything happened to you."

I put my hand over his, where it rested on my cheek.

"Well, tonight you were part of the reason that nothing did happen to me. Mother was worried that I was lonely here and didn't have any friends. But, tonight, I realized how connected I am, to you and the other vampires, to my mother and Margaret and Nyx. Now Meritamun. All of you make me stronger."

He dropped his hand and put his arm around me in a one-armed hug. "That's what friends are for."

CHAPTER 19

Upstairs, Mom had opened the half bottle of whisky that was still left from Hamish's visit. I didn't even like scotch, but I gratefully accepted a small glass.

"Well," my mom said, "I'm glad that's over."

It was such an understatement that we all burst out laughing.

She said, "Meritamun, I don't quite know what we're going to do about you." She glanced at me and I knew that whatever she remembered of this evening, she hadn't forgotten that she had so suddenly embraced her magic. She said, "I'm sure that Lucy and I can manage to get you some identification papers. When my husband and I head back to Egypt, we'd be happy to take you with us, so you could go home."

"Home," she said in a soft voice. "I fear that things have changed since I was last free. All my friends and family are long gone, the only friend I have in the world is Lucy." She glanced at me. "In my world, in my time, I was a servant to a powerful and good magician." She put her hands together and bowed her head slightly. "I would be honored if you would accept me into your service."

I was so stunned, I didn't know what to say. I was about to tell her that slavery had been abolished long ago, but I didn't want to reject her lovely offer. Besides, where would she go? She couldn't begin to imagine how much the world had changed. Before I could speak, Rafe began to chuckle. I could count on the fingers of one hand the number of times I had heard the man laugh, so I couldn't help but stare.

He said, the laughter not quite leaving his face, "Well, you do have an opening for an assistant, Lucy."

I slapped my hand onto my forehead and groaned. "Oh, no, you're right. I've just lost another assistant. I cannot, simply cannot, go back to Mrs. Winters and put up another advert in her shop. I can't take any more lectures about the importance of keeping staff."

Meritamun was looking from one of us to the other with a slightly puzzled expression. I looked over at Mom and then at Margaret and Pete. "What do you think?"

My mother said, "I'd be happier knowing Meritamun was here. For both your sakes. You can look after each other."

I nodded. "It's a great idea. And I have another one. Can we call you Meri?"

"Meri," she rolled the word around her mouth like a sweet. "Meri."

"It sounds more contemporary, and will be easier for people here to say."

"Yes. I like it. A new name for my new life."

Margaret said, "You'd both be welcome into the coven." She saw my expression and said, "Oh, don't worry. Meri is merely an exchange student from Egypt. We might as well stick close to the truth. We'll say she has an expertise in the history of ancient Egypt."

Rafe nodded. "That's an excellent idea, Margaret. Meri is an archaeology student. She's finished her studies, and met Lucy through her parents, which is quite true. Lucy needed an assistant in her knitting shop." Once more, a very uncharacteristic grin spread over his face. "Because her last one exploded in a ball of fire." He was just close enough that I could reach his ankle with my foot, and I kicked him. He laughed aloud again.

Margaret rose. "I must go. However, Lucy, I hope you've learned the importance of community." She drilled me with her bright blue gaze. "Samhain is nearly on us. I expect you both at the Samhain celebration, to be followed by supper."

Mom looked up at that. "May I come, as well?"

Margaret said, "It's certainly time. And now I must go. Blessed be."

After Margaret left, Pete said, "That's all very well, but Meri can't go around a knitting shop, looking like that."

We all looked at Meri's robes and Mom said, "Quick, before your father gets home. You must have something that will fit her?"

I rose and suggested that Meri come with me to my bedroom. We went upstairs and I dug out some old sweatpants and the smallest T-shirt I could find. I said, "We'll go shopping tomorrow and get you some proper clothes."

When I'd helped her put the clothes on and taken out her elaborate hairstyle and combed her long dark hair so it swung straight around her shoulders, she looked very much like a student.

When we got back into the sitting room, my dad had returned home.

I sat on the sofa, and Meri settled nervously at my side, clearly feeling self-conscious in her new clothes. Nyx jumped onto my lap and curled up. She'd barely left my side since we'd all nearly been destroyed.

Pete leaned over and said to Meri, "You look beautiful." Then he colored and said, "I mean, you'll fit right in, with your hair down and those new clothes."

My dad seemed slightly surprised to find an impromptu party going on, but Mom explained that we were celebrating me hiring a new assistant.

My dad looked puzzled. "But what happened to that lovely older woman? She seemed perfect?"

Mom said, smoothly, "She had an emergency with one of her grandchildren. That's why she couldn't give Lucy any notice. But, fortunately, Pete here, knew Meri. She's an expert in the Middle Kingdom."

"Are you?" My dad asked, looking much more interested than he ever had when he'd been conversing with Eileen. "No doubt you went to Cairo University. They do an excellent job, there. It's funny you should appear, because Hamish and I were puzzling over something this evening at dinner. Perhaps you can help us. It concerns Intef the Elder."

"Mom," I whispered. "Stop him."

But she only smiled and shook her head. And, she was right. As Meri and my dad discussed a world she knew so well, she lost her shyness and perhaps regained some of what she'd lost—her history, her family's story.

After she'd answered his question and a few more, he

turned to me. "I have to hand it to you, Lucy. You hired an excellent assistant."

I doubted very much that Meri even knew how to knit. She'd never seen a computer, or lived through an Oxford winter. But, whether he knew it or not, my dad was right. Having a loyal witch as my assistant was going to be a big improvement on a soul-sucking demon.

Rafe said, as though he'd read my mind, "You're right, sir. Loyalty is more important than knowing how to knit." He raised his glass. "I propose a toast to Lucy, and her new assistant."

As everyone raised their glass and repeated the toast, Rafe looked at me, and I knew that Meri wasn't the only one who was pledging me her complete loyalty.

Thanks for reading *Crochet and Cauldrons.* I hope you'll consider leaving a review, it really helps.

Keep reading for a sneak peek of the next mystery, *Stockings and Spells,* the Vampire Knitting Club Book 4.

Stockings and Spells, Chapter 1

AT TEN O'CLOCK, the four of us went downstairs to join the vampire knitting club in the back room of my shop. About fifteen vampires showed up, either coming up through the trapdoor from their underground apartment complex, which was accessed through the tunnel that ran under my shop, or walking in through the shop door. They were happy to see Sylvia and Gran and, after everyone was settled and the knitting needles were flying at warp speed, the crochet hooks traveling so fast they looked like tiny firework displays, I settled to my own knitting. These knitters, who had been practicing their craft for hundreds of years, would put any modern knitter to shame. Still, they very kindly encouraged me, and I kept trying.

We always chatted and gossiped while we worked, but I could feel a strange suppressed energy in the group. I had a feeling they had something on their collective minds, but, I decided not to ask. Probably, whatever it was, I didn't want to know.

We knitted on.

Finally, Alfred said, "Lucy? There's something we want to discuss with you."

Yep, here it came. I'd seen them glancing amongst themselves and clearly Alfred had been nominated to bring up whatever subject they were keen to discuss. "What is it?" I asked.

"We've been thinking, we'd like to have a booth at the Oxford holiday market, this year."

I was so surprised, I dropped my knitting. I think a stitch or two came off the needle but I couldn't worry about that now. I picked up my square. For some reason, it looked like a bent triangle, something like a taco chip in shape. I glanced around at all the eager faces looking at me. "You want to do what?"

Alfred chuckled. "I thought you'd be surprised." He held up his hand, like a magician about to pull a rabbit out of a hat. "Think about it. We have so many knitted garments piling up, we need to get rid of some of them. Also, look how popular our knitted Christmas stockings have been. We've got plenty of goods to stock one of those nice little chalets in the center of town."

"But who's going to sell the stuff?" I asked.

He looked at me as though I were stupid. "We will, of course."

I don't know why I thought this was a terrible idea, but I thought it was a terrible idea. The vampires stayed out of sight, slipped quietly through this ancient city in the shadows. The Oxford holiday market brought shoppers from far and wide and they'd be in the middle of town.

I looked around. "Have you ever been to one of these markets? Do you know how crowded they get?" I didn't want to bring up the notion that all that hot pulsing blood so close to them might be too much of a temptation. They lived off a private blood bank, but I had to assume that it tasted better fresh. Plus, didn't they have an instinct to kill?

Alfred looked a little hurt, as though he'd read my mind. "We want to help."

"Help who?"

"*Whom*, dear," Gran said, without looking up.

"We want to inspire people to take up handicrafts. In the time we've all roamed the earth, people have moved faster and faster, worked longer hours. Now, with modern technology, everyone is 'connected.'" He put air quotes around the word 'connected.' He shook his head. "I worry about people today. They have so much stress and so little leisure time. Knitting is relaxing, and, we'll give all the profits to charity."

I knew that every generation pretty much thought the

next one was doomed. I didn't realize it worked in vampire world as well. It was sweet that they cared about the stresses of modern human life and wanted to alleviate them. Frightening, but sweet.

They could have gone ahead and got a booth without me, but, I suspected they needed my help. So, I reminded them that I was busy running my own shop.

Alfred waved that objection away. "You won't have to do anything, Lucy, just rent the booth in your name, and be the contact person."

Dr. Christopher Weaver, who ran the private blood bank, said, "And, perhaps, you could help with publicity. For instance, you could hang up our poster in your shop window."

They had a poster? "You're serious about this?" I looked around. "Does Rafe know what you're planning?"

Rafe Crosyer was their unofficial leader. I considered him a friend, but he could be very high-handed, and they would never take on an enterprise like this without his tacit permission. They all nodded in unison. "Oh yes," Alfred confirmed. "Rafe is solidly on board."

I looked at Sylvia and Gran, who had been away and, presumably, not part of the conversation. "What do you think?"

Gran smiled her sweet smile. "I think it would be lovely to be involved in a knitting shop again, even if it was only a temporary one. Though, I suppose, I wouldn't be allowed to sit in the booth and sell things."

The very idea made my skin break out in a cold sweat. Gran had been well known in this town before she passed and I had trouble as it was keeping her out of the shop in the middle of the day, when she tended to sleepwalk. We couldn't have her selling scarves at the Christmas market. People from her former life would be bound to notice.

Sylvia glanced quickly at me and then reached over and patted Gran on her shoulder. "We'll need you to manage all the inventory, and, I know it's a lot to ask, but perhaps you could also do the accounting."

Gran, who'd looked downcast when she realized she wouldn't be on the selling floor, brightened up at the idea of being so useful. She nodded. "Yes, that's an excellent idea, Sylvia. I'd be happy to manage the back end of the enterprise."

I couldn't think of any more objections. The ones I had were vague and unformed. I wished Rafe were here, and wondered why he wasn't. Even Meri looked excited at the idea. "I have heard much about this holiday called Christmas. I look forward to seeing it with my own eyes."

I nodded. "I'll see about getting a booth. Though, we could be too late." In fact, the more I thought about it, I imagined you had to book booths months in advance.

Once more they all glanced at each other and looked sheepish. Alfred said, "Actually, you already did."

I felt my forehead wrinkle in puzzlement. "I did what?"

"You may have already made the application and filled out the forms. I believe you've already sent the committee a deposit."

I couldn't be bothered to get annoyed, what was the point? Clearly, they were using me as the front for this enterprise, and clearly I was going to let them. I rolled my eyes. "All right. Tell me what I have to do."

"You have to go tomorrow to the stallholders meeting."

"Were you planning to tell me?" If I hadn't been needed to show my face at this meeting, I wondered if they would have just gone ahead and had this knitting booth in my name, without informing me. They all spoke at once assuring me that they would never do anything I didn't like, but I wasn't too sure.

Order your copy today! *Stockings and Spells* is Book 4 in the Vampire Knitting Club series.

A Note from Nancy

Dear Reader,

Thank you for reading the Vampire Knitting Club series. I am so grateful for all the enthusiasm this series has received.

I hope you'll consider leaving a review and please tell your friends who like cozy mysteries.

Review on Amazon, Goodreads or BookBub.

Your support is the wool that helps me knit up these yarns.

Join my newsletter for a free prequel, *Tangles and Treasons*, the exciting tale of how the gorgeous Rafe Crosyer was turned into a vampire.

I hope to see you in my private Facebook Group. It's a lot of fun. www.facebook.com/groups/NancyWarrenKnitwits

Until next time,
Happy Reading,

Nancy

The best way to keep up with new releases, plus enjoy bonus content and prizes is to join Nancy's newsletter at NancyWarrenAuthor.com or join her in her private Facebook group Nancy Warren's Knitwits.

Vampire Knitting Club: Paranormal Cozy Mystery

Tangles and Treasons - a free prequel for Nancy's newsletter subscribers

The Vampire Knitting Club - Book 1

Stitches and Witches - Book 2

Crochet and Cauldrons - Book 3

Stockings and Spells - Book 4

Purls and Potions - Book 5

Fair Isle and Fortunes - Book 6

Lace and Lies - Book 7

Bobbles and Broomsticks - Book 8

Popcorn and Poltergeists - Book 9

Garters and Gargoyles - Book 10

Diamonds and Daggers - Book 11

Herringbones and Hexes - Book 12

Ribbing and Runes - Book 13

Mosaics and Magic - Book 14

Cat's Paws and Curses - A Holiday Whodunnit

Vampire Knitting Club Boxed Set: Books 1-3

Vampire Knitting Club Boxed Set: Books 4-6

Vampire Knitting Club Boxed Set: Books 7-9

Vampire Knitting Club Boxed Set: Books 10-12

Village Flower Shop: Paranormal Cozy Mystery

Peony Dreadful - Book 1

Karma Camellia - Book 2

Highway to Hellebore - Book 3

The Great Witches Baking Show: Culinary Cozy Mystery

The Great Witches Baking Show - Book 1

Baker's Coven - Book 2

A Rolling Scone - Book 3

A Bundt Instrument - Book 4

Blood, Sweat and Tiers - Book 5

Crumbs and Misdemeanors - Book 6

A Cream of Passion - Book 7

Cakes and Pains - Book 8

Whisk and Reward - Book 9

Gingerdead House - A Holiday Whodunnit

The Great Witches Baking Show Boxed Set: Books 1-3

The Great Witches Baking Show Boxed Set: Books 4-6 (includes bonus novella)

The Great Witches Baking Show Boxed Set: Books 7-9

Vampire Book Club: Paranormal Women's Fiction Cozy Mystery

Crossing the Lines - Prequel

The Vampire Book Club - Book 1

Chapter and Curse - Book 2

A Spelling Mistake - Book 3

A Poisonous Review - Book 4

Toni Diamond Mysteries

Toni is a successful saleswoman for Lady Bianca Cosmetics in this series of humorous cozy mysteries.

Frosted Shadow - Book 1

Ultimate Concealer - Book 2

Midnight Shimmer - Book 3

A Diamond Choker For Christmas - A Holiday Whodunnit

Toni Diamond Mysteries Boxed Set: Books 1-4

The Almost Wives Club: Contemporary Romantic Comedy

An enchanted wedding dress is a matchmaker in this series of romantic comedies where five runaway brides find out who the best men really are!

The Almost Wives Club: Kate - Book 1

Secondhand Bride - Book 2

Bridesmaid for Hire - Book 3

The Wedding Flight - Book 4

If the Dress Fits - Book 5

The Almost Wives Club Boxed Set: Books 1-5

Take a Chance: Contemporary Romance

Meet the Chance family, a cobbled together family of eleven kids who are all grown up and finding their ways in life and love.

Chance Encounter - Prequel

Kiss a Girl in the Rain - Book 1

Iris in Bloom - Book 2

Blueprint for a Kiss - Book 3

Every Rose - Book 4

Love to Go - Book 5

The Sheriff's Sweet Surrender - Book 6

The Daisy Game - Book 7

Take a Chance Boxed Set: Prequel and Books 1-3

Abigail Dixon Mysteries: 1920s Cozy Historical Mystery

In 1920s Paris everything is très chic, except murder.

Death of a Flapper - Book 1

For a complete list of books, check out Nancy's website at NancyWarrenAuthor.com

ABOUT THE AUTHOR

Nancy Warren is the USA Today Bestselling author of more than 100 novels. She's originally from Vancouver, Canada, though she tends to wander and has lived in England, Italy and California at various times. While living in Oxford she dreamed up The Vampire Knitting Club. Favorite moments include being the answer to a crossword puzzle clue in Canada's National Post newspaper, being featured on the front page of the New York Times when her book Speed Dating launched Harlequin's NASCAR series, and being nominated three times for Romance Writers of America's RITA award. She has an MA in Creative Writing from Bath Spa University. She's an avid hiker, loves chocolate and most of all, loves to hear from readers!

The best way to stay in touch is to sign up for Nancy's newsletter at NancyWarrenAuthor.com or join her private Facebook group facebook.com/groups/NancyWarrenKnitwits

To learn more about Nancy and her books
NancyWarrenAuthor.com

Made in the USA
Las Vegas, NV
17 October 2023

79269065R00129